The Topped Toff
By
Louy Castonguay

Copyright © by Louy Castonguay. **ALL** Rights reserved Printed in the US. No part of this book may be used or reproduced in any manner whatsoever without written permission except in the case of brief quotations embodied in critical articles or reviews.

Cover by Get Covers

This is a work of fiction. Any resemblance to any real people is accidental

The Lakeside Dower House
The Topped Toff
Chapter 1

It was dusty looking even from the outside, and huge. The paint was a faded yellow and the enormous amount of windows reflected the lake. Shrubs and weeds and long branches bracketed the house. When Annie turned around, the vista was stunning. The sparkling lake winked and blinked a kaleidoscope reflection of the azure sky.

The world seemed to vibrate to the tune of the birds and squirrels and the waves gently lapping the sandy beach not far from the house. She caught her breath, amazed by the beauty. Why was this gorgeous place abandoned?

She'd been raised by two middle class parents who encouraged her in her chosen field of finance, paid for her schooling and helped her get her first apartment in the city. They never ever spoke of great aunt Kelly Marie. Who was this maiden aunt of her mother, and why had she left her house to Annie? How had her great aunt acquired it? Why had she left it to her, of all people?

Her parents died together, as they might have wished. Their car was hit by a falling tree, of all things. She had no siblings, and she knew of no other relatives. That is, she didn't until she received the letter from a law office here in Abigale, Maine.

Dear Mrs. Carlton

"You are a hard person to find.

Louy Castonguay

I was wrapping up my father's law practice and found a folder with your name, the name of your parents and that they are deceased. My sympathies. We've been looking for you for a few years.

Your great-aunt Kelly Marie Weeks has passed, also. She left her possessions to you specifically. Her house in Abigale, Maine is yours, now, as are all her assets, with only one condition. You must live in the house for six months. At that time, her full holdings will pass to you.

The indications are that there are no other relatives. Please contact us as soon as possible.

When the pandemic hit, her job in finance in New York went away.

Out of boredom and idleness, she was sorting things in her to do file in her desk and rediscovered the letter. The letterhead was for a law firm called Peters Brothers Law. The address and phone number at the top of the letterhead were crossed out. She'd thought it was one of those scams. Give us $50 to redeem your inheritance or something along those lines. A phone number and an address were at the bottom of the letter. She had parked the letter with some other correspondence she meant to get to.

When she dialed the number and got a voice mail, she played along, just to see what would happen. She left a message, and she stated she had no money to give to this scam and angrily hung up.

An hour later, her phone had rung. "Mrs. Carlton? Mrs. Annie Carlton?"

"That's Miss, but yes. Who is this?"

"Ah, finally. We've been looking for you." This echoed what had been in the letter and she thought she might be speaking to the person who wrote it.

"What is this about?"

"I'm Tom Junior. Ah, Tom Peters Junior. I wrote you about your great aunt's will."

"Yes. I see that. I'm sorry. I've been otherwise occupied." She wanted to see what the scam was.

"I didn't know her well, though my dad did, and my grandfather, too. But it seems your great aunt thought highly of you. If you don't claim the estate, the instructions are that it will be sold off and the proceeds donated to a woman's shelter or something like that. I'd have to refresh myself on the details. I do remember that to gain access to the whole inheritance, you have to move in and live there for six months." He stopped talking.

Annie didn't know what to say.

Finally, he spoke again. "Look, this is a nice place that could do with a bit of a fix up. And I can tell you the bequest is sizeable. If you come on down, I can go into details with you, though there are facts I don't have access to. Are you up for a trip to Maine?"

"Sure. What the heck. I have nothing else going on. They've opened interstate travel again. I can be there next weekend, I think."

"Excellent. I'll see you then." He gave her the address of his place, which matched the address on the letter. "You have GPS, I take it?"

After she said yes, he hung up before she could ask any more questions.

"Well, going to Maine, I guess," she said to the four walls of her apartment. She brought out her laptop and started a search, first for Abigale, Maine, then the Peters Brothers Law. Next, she googled the supposed great aunt's name.

Abigale was easy to find, and actually had paved roads going to it, which she felt relieved about. Peters Brothers Law had no listing. She then went looking for any news posting. She found an obituary for Eldred Peters, who had died eight years ago. He left a son, Thomas, and his wife and a brother who were previously deceased. So much for that. At least there had *been* a Peters Brothers Law.

She was expected to arrive Saturday and meet with Thomas Peters Junior Saturday afternoon. She'd opted to travel up early, incognito, and scope things out. All things considered, there was nothing better to do, and besides, funds were getting low, even with unemployment. Maybe she could find work in Maine. Did they even have an economy in Maine?

She packed and left the next day, a gorgeous late summer Wednesday. Her google map told her it would take six hours to get to Abigale from New York. Her longest trips had been to her parents in New Jersey, which took two hours.

She left the city before rush hour with a grand sense of adventure. Whatever she found in Maine, it had to be better than just sitting in her apartment waiting to go dead flat broke. At least she'd see some country. She pictured

Maine as all seashore and woods. Was Abigale near the seashore, or deep in the woods?

After two and half hours, she couldn't drive anymore and needed a break. At the Massachusetts border, she came to realize there was so much distance in the states. You could cross Jersey in a few hours. This was a bigger project than she'd thought. She pulled over to a tourist stop, fueled up, got an early lunch and coffee.

The rest stop was almost deserted. It was set up to handle many more people. Maybe on weekends it was busier. Some people were still masked up, decreasing conversations to the essentials. She took her time over her lunch and climbed back in the car.

Energized, she found she was looking forward to whatever Abigale, Maine held for her. If she could find work. she could make the move up there permanent, that is if this wasn't an elaborate scam. Humming, then singing along with the radio, she drove another two hours before she crossed a huge bridge into Maine. It was like a gateway. Even the air felt different. She saw seagulls, smelled tidal flats, and saw a fair number of cars from other states all going in the same direction as herself, north.

She stopped once more in a place she couldn't pronounce that started with a K and had lots of consonants. Ken something. The fast-food servers were chattier than at the previous rest stop. However, no one knew anything about her destination. She spent a bit of time at the rest stop, with her laptop looking up the town statistics. It was a small town of five thousand people, had a high school, middle school, and an elementary school, too. She googled

Main Street and took a virtual tour of the town. It looked like it was stuck in the fifties.

As she closed her laptop and headed for her car, she took a moment to wonder what she was getting herself into. But anything would be better than stagnating in her tiny apartment in the city, surrounded by other folks who were also bewildered by the recent events. Predictions about the economy were dire.

Finally, she arrived and walked around a property that somebody was saying was hers. It was a different world. She'd had several outdoor trips with her father, seeking great photos with expensive cameras, fishing in rental boats at rustic lodges, but more often just hanging out at seaside beaches for a day. Once, the family had rented a camp for a week. Her mother had hated it. Another year, her parents had enrolled her at summer camp for two weeks.

As she got older, the trips got less frequent as other activities took up her time. Windy high-rise city streets became her 'outdoors'.

Here, she was surrounded by nature. A lake at her feet, woods behind her, and a big mausoleum of a house were very far from the surroundings she was accustomed to. This had to be a scam. This big, old, deserted property was being used as a magnet for naïve individuals. She double-checked the address given in the letter.

As she looked at the building, she mentally cut it up. If each set of windows were one apartment, like in the city, where space was at a premium, dozens of apartments could fit in here. Dozens. She wandered the grounds for a time, wishing she'd worn different shoes. The heels of her suede

The Topped Toff

boots sunk in the soft earth. She looked in a few of the windows and saw nothing but rooms that seemed empty. She walked to the beach and sat on a root. The sparkling water mesmerized her.

She saw a family of ducks swimming only a few feet from her. The water was so clear she could see their feet paddling below the surface and now understood better the reference she'd heard so many times about being like a duck, calm on the surface, gliding along, but paddling like crazy below the surface. That's how she'd always felt in her fast-paced world. Finance. It had been music to her ears all through school, like a holy grail.

And then she'd finally gotten a job! Sitting here, on a root, she realized she didn't want to go back to working with numbers, mindlessly transposing them from one place to another. Most people in finance were just dressed-up pencil pushers. She enjoyed the puzzle of numbers, but it would be years and years before she was senior enough to lead a team.

With a sigh, she stood. She walked back to her car, knowing something fundamental had shifted inside her. Maybe she was disillusioned with economics, which had seemed so grand to her younger self. Whatever the future held, things would never go back to what they had been. She might just live out her life here, as had her supposed Great Aunt Kelly Marie. Even the name sang of independence and freedom.

She found a bed and breakfast outside of town and got registered and found her room. It would do. She wanted to explore the area without anyone knowing her mission. She had to travel a bit to find a place for supper. After she got back to her room, she took out her laptop and explored Abigale and the surrounding area again. She found listings for the library, grocery store, hardware store, a State Farm Office, a theater and more. It seemed a proper little town.

The lake sparkled in her dreams all night long. The morning was a different story, as it was drizzly and dark. She loitered in her room until an unreasonable hour before showering, styling her hair and putting on her makeup for the day. She then went out to find some lunch, having missed breakfast at the bed and breakfast. She reflected that she was getting good at this idling business. All her life she'd had goals, a new benchmark to reach, extra credits in high school and in college, extra hours put in at work to acquire a great reputation as a hard worker. She recognized that was now all in the past. She wondered what *the legacy* amounted to. With her luck, it was just bills and back taxes. On the other hand, she might never have to work again. As she drove around town, looking for a Starbucks or other coffee shop, she was brought near to tears.

Her natural shyness kept her in the car rather than getting out and talking with locals. She grabbed the door handle three times to open the car door, then pulled back.

She didn't want the Peters person to know she was in town. Would she be able to learn something about this mysterious aunt she hadn't known about?

After she'd gone by Josie's Inn and Cafe four times, she stopped and parked. Once inside, she found Josie's Inn was a delightful and small place. She ordered the Rueban and an iced tea. The waitress was chatty.

The Topped Toff   9

"I see there's a big old house just outside of town. A huge thing with yellow paint."

"Yes. The Lakehouse or the Dower, depending on who you ask."

"Tell me about it, if you can."

"Yes. I can." She looked around. The restaurant was almost empty. She sat across from Annie.

"So, I didn't know her. She was an old recluse, apparently. She inherited it from her mother, who got it, I'm told from an unfaithful husband. I'm not sure if that's true." She cast her eye once more around the restaurant, then relaxed into her seat. "What I do know is that during the twenties and thirties, it served as a Lakehouse. That's a sort of inn for the fancy folks to come for the summer. There were wild parties, lots of booze, even during the Great Depression and during Prohibition."

"Sounds like a great place. Who owns it now. It looks abandoned."

"Oh, the old lady who lived there died. She left it to some distant relative. Tom has been trying to get ahold of that person for ages."

"Oh." Annie went speechless. Apparently, the woman knew Tom personally. It was an indication that small towns were intimate, and she'd have to be careful.

"So, wild parties, an inn, sort of, but it's a beautiful setting."

"Yes. Lots of folks have tried to buy it over the years. Miss Kelly didn't wat to sell. Said she was keeping it for a special person. I hear that person is going to show up here this weekend. It's a city person. I'll bet she'll take one look at the huge old tumble of a mansion and put it on the market. Lots of folks would love to get their hands on it, including some developers who want to knock it down and build high-end retirement condos." The waitress rattled on about the various groups and individuals that wanted it. "I'm told it's worth a million dollars, because it comes with lots of land, and then I'm told it's worth almost nothing, since it's so old and in need of so much care. But that might just be someone trying to low ball. We could do with some injection of money in this town, so condos catering to the rich would be nice." Once again, she looked over to see if the few people in the Café needed anything and turned back to Annie. "It is a great place, too, with a nice sandy beach. The EPA won't let you construct beaches anymore, so the ones that exist are pretty special."

The EPA must be some sort of government agency. She allowed the waitress to continue spieling on about the issues of the town as she recalled the dazzling view of lake she'd seen yesterday.

Someone entered the door of the eatery.

"Sorry. Gotta go. Tom is often in a hurry. Hey, stop on by again, if you will be in town for long." She stood elegantly and went to wait on the customer.

Annie wondered if this was Tom Peters Jr. or another Tom. She finished her lukewarm coffee and left money to cover her bill and a generous tip and was reminded that her funds were dropping dangerously low. If she gave up her apartment, if she didn't have to pay rent, if she moved into that huge old house, she'd be able to weather the

The Topped Toff

continuing economic crisis until she decided what to do next. She wondered what the unemployment benefits were like in Maine.

As she left the restaurant, almost unconsciously, she was stripping her apartment, sorting what she'd bring to Maine, and deciding what to get rid of, and if she really wanted to move into a house that would accommodate all of her friends for a wild weekend, like days of old.

☰ ☰ ☰

Dower Chapter 2

Brunch at the Village Inn, luck of the draw supper at the inn, and two days wandering the countryside gave Annie a feel for the area. Bangor, what passed for a city in this rural state, seemed to be a hub for the surrounding smaller towns. It had a large hospital, several box grocery stores, and some congregate shopping centers with nationally known chains and restaurants.

Saturday arrived and she felt on edge as she thought about meeting with 'Tom' and learning details about the legacy supposedly left to her. She'd had time to think about the large old house on the edge of a lake just outside a tiny little town off the beaten path, although she still considered that this might all be an elaborate scam. She'd thought about the parties she could throw here although her friends were all in New York and probably wouldn't travel here just for some fun. They weren't real friends, anyway, just someone at work and to hang out with in any spare time any of them had. No one was close enough to share the current development in her life.

Finally, the appointed time arrived. She'd scoped out the building where she was supposed to meet Tom. It was a big old Victorian, similar to the house that had been left to her, but smaller by a lot.

She rang the doorbell, attempting to appear confident and sure of herself, while trying to think of a brilliant opening line, something she'd often done in her previous world.

She was nervously clearing her throat when a casually dressed, and trim individual opened the door.

The Topped Toff

"Ah, you must be Annie." He opened the door wider and stepped back. "Come in, come in. Please."

It was indeed *the* Tom from the restaurant. "Thank you," she choked out, as she walked in.

The foyer was huge, almost as big as her entire New York apartment. She found she was gazing around her as if lost in the woods. Everywhere she looked there were adornments from past eras, trinkets and pictures and a huge chandelier.

"Right this way. Joe will be handling things for you. He's the lawyer who took over from Dad."

"Oh. I had thought you were the one." She thought, from her research, that Tom had taken on his father's practice.

He chuckled and shook his head. "Me. I'm not lawyer material."

She followed Tom into a room lined with books. Her head swiveled around at the four walls. Only one wall had no books, and that wall had two widely spaced and lushly draped windows and a large landscape painting between the windows. She didn't have a chance to gaze at the painting.

"This is Joe Johnson. He will handle the estate for you. I'm just an observer, a facilitator, if you will."

Joe stood up from behind a massive antique desk and walked up to Annie and put his hand out for a handshake, then immediately pulled it back. "Sorry. I keep forgetting the Covid restrictions." He then pulled up the mask that had been hanging around his neck. He returned to his seat and folded his tall lean body into the space between chair and desk. He opened a folder in front of him. "So, did you know your aunty well?"

Annie had stopped wearing her mask a few months ago. "No, not at all. As a matter of fact, I didn't even know she existed. Was she on my dad's side or mom's?"

"Oh, I thought you'd known her, since she left you the house and the endowment with it,"

"Exactly what do you mean by the endowment?"

"We'll get to that. And in answer to your question, she was related to your mother. Your grandmother Louise, Kelly Marie's sister, was from Abigale. How much of this do you know?"

"Nothing. I know nothing." Annie was still suspicious of the entire proceedings, wondering at what point the 'scam' would pull the trigger to try to get into her bank account.

"We know that your grandmother, Louise Weeks Smith, left and never moved back. After your great aunt, Kelly Marie Weeks, died, we have been looking for your mother. "We finally found your mother's married name in your great grandmother Anita's obituary. But then we weren't able to find her." He nodded at her and held her gaze for a moment. "I'm sorry for your loss, by the way."

"Thank you."

Tom spoke up. "After we learned your parents had died, we couldn't find you. That is until very recently. When we didn't hear back, we thought maybe the letter got lost, or maybe you'd moved, what with everything going on."

Annie sat and listened. Joe was about the same age as Tom, she thought. Both were notably handsome but dressed

The Topped Toff 15

casually. She thought they would both look fairly sharp dressed in suits with stylish ties. Maybe standards were more relaxed in the country.

Tom spoke up. "Man, I was afraid I was going to have to go into the city and search for you. Time was running out on this. Searches were simpler, in Dad's days, with telephone directories. Now everyone has a cell phone."

Annie still suspected a scam but was willing to give the two the benefit of the doubt.

Joe continued. "We'll eventually have to see some confirming ID, or course, but that can wait."

"What is this endowment you speak of."

"I know that Kelly Marie Weeks left very specific instructions."

Annie was struck by the depths of his very blue eyes. Tom also had blue eyes, but of a lighter shade and she idly wondered if they might be related.

"You get the house. There is an endowment attached, which was put in place by the original person who bought it for his wife as a wedding gift. Women weren't considered able to own property, back then. That person would have been your great great grandmother." He checked the papers in front of him. "Yes, that's right. The amount is not as great as it used to be, due to inflation. It is handled by the lawyer in charge, which is currently me, and can only be used for things like repairs, taxes, maintenance, and such. You can't touch the principle. Tom here, has been mowing lawns and checking on it from time to time"

My pleasure," said Tom, seated beside Annie.

She looked over at Tom. "Oh, you've been looking after it?" Her focus returned to Joe.

"I asked him to, after the matter fell into my hands." Joe glanced down at the paperwork and quickly looked back at Annie. "Also, there is a current account besides the endowment In case you do not move in, all this will get dissolved, and the money will get donated to a special fund for homeless women."

He looked up at Annie, then glanced at Tom before studying the paperwork on his desk. "Over the last few years, the fund has grown a bit since no one has used it. You don't get any of the income until you've lived there six months.""

Annie smiled at Tom, then at Joe. Again, she was struck by the resemblance, not so much in the face as in the body type, dress and demeanor. "Go on."

"Let's see. It was originally bought for your great grandmother Anita Guay Weeks by her husband Lucien Weeks. Some say---. Well, that's just gossip and from a long time ago. She had three children. A boy, Peter, died in childhood. Your grandmother Louise and her sister Kelly Marie, lived here until your grandmother moved away, but Kelly Marie stayed. We've been trying to find Louise for a while."

"What's this we. I don't remember you doing much of it." Tom's smile accompanied his teasing.

"Well, all right. I'll give you that. You owe Tom for finding her obituary.

Tom chuckled. "Obituaries carry great amounts of information, though they can be boring to go through.

Annie nodded. "I never knew my grandmother."

"When we finally found the obituary for your mother only one survivor was listed. You. The house was specifically listed as going to you, by name."

"I never even knew we had relatives. I mean, everyone has ancestors, just that mine were never talked about. I knew Mom came from Maine and Dad came from New Jersey. That's all I knew."

Joe glanced back at the file on his desk, as if to reassure himself, then looked at Annie as he recited the facts. "The house is yours, along with the attached dower endowment, as long as you live in it for six months before 2025, that's ten years after Kelly died. He took a breath and then smiled.

Annie interrupted him. "Why did my mother leave? Why did I not know about great aunt Kelly Marie? Are you sure she was, well, like, related to me?"

Joe answered. "Family stuff can be difficult, sometimes. We knew you'd have lots of questions. We simply don't know. Louise went away and we don't think she ever came back to town." He paused.

"Go on," said Annie.

"She was a wealthy woman. No one is sure where the money came from. Some say it was garnered during prohibition by her grandparents, some say she had a wealthy paramour, others say it was left by Lucien as a guilt offering to Anita after the death of the boy Peter. We do know that Lucien would sometimes come to visit her, but he never actually lived here. From what we've heard, Anita seems to have raised the girls on her own."

Tom took up the narrative. "We did do due diligence." He looked at Joe. "By that I mean, I did. I talked to almost many an old timer who might have known them. The Weeks didn't mingle with the locals and apparently kept to themselves after leaving school. Kelly had lots of friends, it seems, but none of them were from Abigale. She had some pretty flashy parties, but always with people from somewhere else. Aside from grocery delivery and the like, no one from town went to the house."

Joe picked up the conversation, pointing to the file on the desk. "In any case, Kelly Marie was aware of you, her niece's child, and she charged Peters and Sons with endowing you with the house." He checked the papers on the desk again, though he seemed to already know what was there. "As I already said, there's the building trust to care for the property but there's more. There is a sealed trust, which will come to you after six months, with stocks in a portfolio, of undetermined value, and a cash amount which has been accumulating since her death. We estimate that the value of house, stocks and cash is somewhere around a million."

Annie gasped. She shook her head. "I must have heard wrong. You said what?"

"About a million. That's just a rough estimate. Once you get the inheritance, we'll do a deep dive and get you a real figure, hire you a finance guy, all that."

She was speechless. "All that money. My folks barely scraped by. And why me? Why me specifically?"

"We don't know that. The facts are laid out, but the background is not. It does seem there are no other Weeks descendants." Joe closed the file. "That's it, then? Any more questions? Questions about this?"

Annie sat like a rock, stunned.

Tom laughed. "Anything we can do for you, Miss?"

"I'm rich?"

Joe smiled at her and nodded once. "Yes, you are. If you live in the house for six months. Will that be a problem?"

Annie shook her head no, speechless.

"Let us know if we can be of assistance. I would love to have you as a client, but you can choose any lawyer, of course. As soon as you do, I'll transfer all this to them. You might want one of those high-powered New York firms for something this big."

"Are you saying you aren't able?"

"Oh, no. Not at all. Just, I don't want you to feel you have to stay with a small-town hack."

"I'll have to think about it." Annie stood. "Good day. You've certainly given me something to think about."

"One more thing."

Annie looked puzzled. What more? *Here comes the scam,* she thought.

"I need to see your ID."

Annie looked at him blankly.

"Driver's License? Anything."

Annie showed him her license.

"Here are the keys."

"Oh, of course. Yes." She took the dangled keys from Joe. "Of course. Oh, my gosh. I had no idea." She turned to leave. She then turned back. "I can go live there, now?"

Tom answered with a wide grin. "It's yours. Do what you will, but six months. Can you stand small town living for that long?"

"I'll certainly try." She nodded assent. "I should be able. Oh, my gosh. Yes."

She left the building feeling very unlike herself. "What the heck," she said to herself, as she got into her car. "What the heck."

≡ ≡ ≡

Dower Chapter 3

Annie drove over to Kelly's house, her house now, the Lakeside Dower House. Her mind was reeling from what she'd just learned. This was her house. She only had to live in it for six months.

She sat in her car, gazing out at the sparkling lake. She could enjoy that view all she wanted. She looked up at the house. What was she going to do with all that house? Maybe she'd make it into an inn, a fancy one. Where would she get the money to fix it up, though?

She remembered there was a fund for the house. She hadn't thought to ask how much of it she'd be able to spend. If she stayed here, she'd need to earn somehow.

Her thoughts still swirling, she got out of the car and slowly approached the front door, keys in hand. Time to see what she'd been left by a woman she didn't know. As she turned the key, she took a moment to wonder why her great aunt had left the house to her and not her mother. A mystery to solve, for sure.

She entered a grand foyer, a bit smaller than the one at the lawyer's house, but with more doors leading from it. She counted seven doors. Taking a deep breath, and hoping for no surprises, she stepped to her left and opened the door. It was a huge library, with wall to ceiling shelves, but no books. She wondered if the shelves had ever held books, and if so, where they had gone. Just how many books would fit on these shelves? Two chairs were in the room. When she lifted their sheet coverings, she saw two antique Morrison chairs, a sort of old-fashioned recliner, the cushions covered in red and gold damask. In the middle of the room stood a grand old desk, like in the lawyer's office and an antique swivel rocker chair with cracked leather upholstery. The room was echoey, bouncing back the sound of her high heeled boots to her. No curtains framed the windows.

She moved on to the next room, which was completely empty, but surprisingly clean for an abandoned house.

On one wall, there was an ornamental shelf between two windows, a nicknack shelf, only about 8" inches wide and two feet long. The walls were covered in taupe-colored paper with gold colored cabbage roses. Again, there were no curtains at the large windows. She closed the door and moved on. She found two more empty rooms, vibrant wallpaper in neutral tones but with a spark of vibrant color coated the walls.

The door at the end of the hallway led to a huge kitchen with a six-burner gas stove. She flicked the knobs on to see if the stove worked and then flicked them back off. Multiple cupboards, several closets, broom closets, lots of counter space, an island in the middle, two windows at the far end, a windowed door leading outside, and a refrigerator occupied the kitchen, and a mystery door was located at one end.

When she opened it, she found a walk-in pantry with a much larger refrigerator and a chest type freezer whose lid was propped open. It all seemed clean, too clean for an abandoned house, she thought. Next, she opened cupboards and found no dishes, no pots, no kettles, no glasses, no silverware in the drawers and no linens of any kind. Also, the room held no kitchen table, except a small one off to the side with only two chairs, sort of a workstation, she thought. The table would have been ideal in her apartment in the city but was dwarfed in this house. Would she ever need a room this large?

Inside the next door down she found a formal dining room. A large table with chairs that were upholstered in a fabric that complemented the wallpaper, a break front and a highboy were the only things in the room. Both the breakfront and the highboy were empty. No dishes, no silverware, no linen. The two windows again had no curtains but were sparkling clean.

The next door led to a narrow stairway that went down. She thought she'd leave the cellar for later. She closed the door and moved on.

She went upstairs. A long hallway and seven open doors. All the rooms were empty except for an occasional wooden chair or end table. No beds, no linens, no curtains.

"What the heck" she said to all the emptiness.

She left the doors open behind her after glancing in. The eighth door was closed. She opened it and found a huge room, as big as two of the others. It had two doors inside, which she couldn't get to because of all the furniture crammed into it. There were bed frames, bureaus, old-fashioned clothes wardrobes, a few dressing tables stacked on top of other things and boxes and boxes, piled atop each other in one corner of the room. The room was so stuffed she couldn't get to any of it. It would have to come out in the order it had been put in. She wondered who had jammed all this in here. She detected a faint order of cedar and something else, maybe moth balls.

She headed back downstairs, aware this would take more than a few hours to sort. She'd have to stay at the inn another night or two. The door knocker sounded. She could see through the sidelights that someone was standing outside the door. Wondering who her first visitor was going to be, she went to the door.

"Oh, hi Tom." Her first thought was that this had really been an elaborate scam and now he'd ask for money for something or other and she'd eventually find out that this house belonged to someone else.

"Hi." He seemed uncharacteristically bashful.

"Hi. Need something?"

"Uh, no. I thought you might. Uh, need something. I have a bit of time."

"What?"

"I know you had mentioned moving in. But it's not ready. You won't even have a bed, not tonight, not without some help, anyway. Everything got piled willy-nilly in that upstairs bedroom. I did get the power turned on yesterday, though."

"How do you know what's in there?"

"Didn't I mention? My dad and I had charge of closing it up. By the time we got here, the mice had been having a field day."

"Mice?"

"Mice are these cute cartoony little things. But so destructive."

Annie realized he was still standing on the doorstep, her doorstep. "Do come in. There are several chairs in the kitchen."

The Topped Toff

"I always loved that kitchen. We had to put most of that away, too. First, we had to wash everything. They'd been in all the drawers and cupboards, pooped in all the bowls and plates, and just everything. We piled it all in that room upstairs, the largest, furthest from the ground, and saturated it with cedar and mint and mothballs. I check every now and again, put down new bait in the corners and make sure everything is fine."

"Oh, you did it. I wondered."

"We had help, and they didn't much care how things got upstairs, as long as it all got in there. I think the crew did a fair job, all things considered."

"All things considered," she echoed. She was hung up on the image of mouse droppings.

Tom followed her to the kitchen, and they sat at the only two chairs, across from each other at the small table. "Mice are destructive. They chew everything up, including the insulation on wires, bedclothes, they'll nest in beds, upholstered chairs, anything like that and they multiply like rabbits."

Annie had no idea how rabbits multiplied and just sat, a bit embarrassed by the mention of mouse and rabbit sex, and her own ignorance, waiting to hear the rest of the story, still wondering if this was a scam and they were now trying to get rid of her.

"Mice." She was a bit nervous, too. Her hidden shyness was keeping her from thinking straight.

"Yup. Mice."

Annie finally found something to say. "In New York, we don't have mice. We have rats. And roaches. We have pest control come through once or twice a year and set traps and spray for vermin."

"Yes. Well. Traps and then the cedar and mint. I've heard lavender helps, too. I didn't have any."

"Lavender for mice. Got it."

"Why not stay one more night at your inn. Tomorrow, I'll come help you and we can start to unpack that room, move stuff, set up a bed, get some kitchen stuff out." He paused and watched to see any reaction. "If you like?"

"I like that. Yes." She smiled at him, suddenly feeling like she'd acquired a friend in this strange place with lapping water and mice wanting to take over.

"Good. Say eight o'clock. Get an early start?"

"If we unpack that room, will we find mice in there?"

"I haven't seen any sign in there."

"Won't they just take over, again, if we take everything out?"

"They don't like people. But if you pack cedar, mothballs, mint and lavender in the corners, I think you can keep them out. And maybe get a cat. Or even two."

"I've never had a cat. I know nothing about them."

"They are great mousers."

"Or a dog," she said thoughtfully.

"Some dogs are bred to catch rats, like the chihuahua. I personally like a bigger beefier dog. Each to their own. But cats should do the trick, and they're easier to maintain." He stood. "I'll see myself out and see you in the morning. Mind if I bring a few friends?"

The Topped Toff   27

"I guess." She followed to the door. "Tomorrow, then."

His smile was like sunshine. "Tomorrow." He sprinted down the outside stairs and strode to his car. He waved to her just before getting in and driving off.

She closed the door behind him. "Now what?"

She went back up to the crowded room, looked at the jammed in mess, thought for a moment of starting the unloading, decided that the heavier items put just inside the door would make that impractical, it was getting late, and she could wait until morning.

She sat by the lake for half an hour, listening to the sounds around her. Everything was so different here. How could her grandmother Louise stand to leave? Her grandfather John Smith must have been some sort of man to pull her away. What had happened between the sisters, she wondered. Would she ever find out?

She finally gave up on thinking about the past, her mother, the grandmother she never knew, the great aunt she never knew about, and the interactions among them all. She didn't even know if her mother knew about the mysterious aunt.

Annie moved to Josie's Inn, to be nearer and since she didn't have to be clandestine about her presence. That night, Josie was serving beef stew. "I wanted to serve you pork chops, but I didn't know what time you might wander in. Tom said you'd be along, since the house wasn't ready yet. I've been telling him he needed to get that stuff together. He said the new owner would want it done their own way."

"Thanks." Overwhelmed by her sudden reversal of fortunes, she felt she had no words. Everyone knew about the house but her.

"We didn't even know how old you were, if you were married, or anything. Though Tom did say you still carried your parent's name. If you'd gotten married, we might never have found you. Well, Tom might never have found you." Josie was one of those folks who hated gaps in conversation, and she loved to talk, too.

"I'm grateful for being able to stay here. The house is so bare."

"It was stuffed to the gills, at one time. Absolutely full of stuff, generations of people collecting things, you know." Josie kept Annie company during the meal, coming and going as she served others, giving a bit of history. "There were always lots of folks up there, from away, you know. The weekends were huge, especially in summer. Up until the 1970's I think. After that, things got a little quieter. Then, suddenly, one of the sisters was gone. The other one, your aunt, was really quiet. There were no more visitors, except one, from time to time. The other sister, your grandmother, Louise, she never came here that I know of. Oh, sometimes Kelly'd go off, no one knew where, but never for long, a week at the most."

Josie kept up the patter, not really adding much, just talking while Annie ate her meal.

"That was great. Thanks. And thanks for the information."

"You are welcome."

"I think I'll go lay down. I'm tired. It's been a huge day."

The two women parted, and Annie went to her room.

The Topped Toff

☰   ☰   ☰

Chapter 4

Josie had a light breakfast on the table when Annie came down at seven. Donuts and Danish were on a platter. Annie smelled fresh coffee, too. "Thought you could use a bit of breakfast here before getting out to the house."

"Great. Yes. I'll have one of those Danish. Looks great. I didn't mean to cause you trouble."

"Look, you'll have a long day out there, putting things to right. So, I'll bring supper out to you, if that's all right. I'll bring enough to feed a group, so's anyone that wants to stay to supper can."

Annie eyes widened. It wasn't like this in the city where she'd lived, nor in the city she'd grown up in. "There's no need?"

"Just being neighborly. We do hope you stay. We'd love to see that big old place opened up again."

"We'll see." Annie heart expanded at the unaccustomed friendliness.

She drank a cup and a half of excellent coffee and ate a Danish *and* a donut before getting in her car and going out to meet Tom. She'd worn her oldest jeans, a soft top and flat shoes, thinking of the stairs she'd be up and down all day.

The first thing to catch her eye was the sparkle on the water. It distracted her. She dragged her eyes back to the half a dozen cars parked near the house. The one closest to the house was Tom's

"What the heck?" she asked herself before getting out.

"Hi," greeted Tom. "Ready to go to work?"

The Topped Toff

"I'm ready. What's with all these cars?"

"Oh, just some help I brought along. You said I could." He smiled bashfully.

"Fine. Well, let's get to it. I hope these folks don't expect to get paid. I don't have much money."

"Oh, no. This is just volunteer stuff. No money. Please don't offer any. They'd be insulted."

As the two spoke, eight people got out of five different cars.

First to come up to them was an older couple, both slim, she had grey hair put up in a bun and he had a shaved head showing just a small rim of stubble indicating he was nearly bald before the shave.

"Annie Carlton, meet John and Joanne. They are proud owners of the local hardware store where you'll go for any stuff you need for repairs."

"Good to meet you," said John.

Joanna just nodded her greeting.

And the introductions continued. A grocer, a vet, a vet assistant, a housewife, an accountant and a bank teller. Annie lost track of the names. As she was introduced, she still wondered about it being a scam, wanting to pinch herself. Was this real?

Tom was holding out his hand.

Annie looked at the extended hand, palm up before she realized he wanted the keys. She handed them over.

Tom led the group into the house.

"If you'll come upstairs with me, you can direct where you want stuff brought to, and these folks will get it there for you."

Annie had never worked on a project like this and was fine with Tom taking it over.

"We'll start with the heavy stuff by the door." He opened the door to the large room.

Annie hadn't seen the two wheeled trolley just inside the door of the room on her previous look in.

Tom had suggested she direct where stuff would go, but he remembered where most of it had come from and helped her direct the workers. The men moved heavy furniture and the women worked together to set up rooms.

Item after item went out of the crowded room. Dressers, beds, boxes of linens for the beds, and plastic bags filled with curtains were brought out. Someone found the ironing board in the kitchen and started ironing curtains.

"How much time did you spend in this house? You seem to remember how all the rooms were fixed up."

"Yes. I do. My dad, besides being a lawyer, was handyman to the women folk. He'd bring me along, sometimes. Ah, here comes the kitchen stuff. You might want to have the boxes put in the kitchen so you can place things like you'd want them. We had to throw out some stuff. Most of it is there, though."

Box after box went down to the kitchen. Only a few pieces of furniture, a bed frame and mattress, and some boxes were left.

The Topped Toff   33

"Hey Marc. Can I have that trolley. We have hit bottom. We'll need these last boxes brought to the library. Almost done."

Marc handed over the two-wheel trolley. "Tom. Tell me we won't have to put all these books back."

"No. We'll let the Misses of the estate put them on the shelves, if she decides to keep them."

Marc looked at Annie. "I'll take anything you don't want off your hands. Kelly had some valuable books. Some got destroyed before we got things cleaned up. She sold a few. Well, quite a few, actually. If and when you want to know what you have of any value, I'd be more than glad to take a look."

Annie looked at Marc with a puzzled look. She couldn't remember if he was the grocer or the Vet.

"My wife runs a small online antiquities shop. A hobby of ours, mostly old books. We love them, but can't keep them all, so we buy and sell. Man, the space downstairs would serve as a beautiful sales space."

Annie thought of offering the use of the library to them, rethought it before she opened her mouth. It might be something to consider. Did she want people walking into her home?

By midafternoon, curtains were hung, four beds set up and made up with sheets and coverlets, end tables, as well as a sofa and end chairs, and more had been set up in various rooms and the large upstairs bedroom had been emptied of all but the original bedroom furniture.

Tom walked Annie through the house. "This was Kelly's bedroom. This room may have been her sister's room. It was always kept pristine, but no one had used it in a coon's age. This next room was always empty, as far back as I can recall."

She saw a room set up as a living room, a parlor, Tom called it. "This room was her office, but she had the desk moved to the library in her last years here. That's why it's now empty. And this room was a maid's room, I think, back in the day."

Some of the folks had bid good day and left. Only John and Joanne and Tom were left. They were standing in the hallway when there was a knock on the door

Tom turned to open it.

Annie slapped her forehead. "I forgot. Josie said she was bringing supper. I'm not sure what it is, but would you like to stay?"

All three said yes, as Josie entered, loaded down with several shopping bags.

"Here, let me." Tom was taking things from her.

"I made China Pie. That's what Ma called it, anyways." Josie pattered on. "Seems when the Chinese were building railroad, they were served this, or maybe it was one of the first meals being served on the diner cars, or some version of that. In any case, it is still warm. I've brought along plates and forks, in case you haven't found your kitchen stuff yet, and you won't need to do dishes, either. My, looks great." She followed Tom and Annie into the kitchen. "Oh, just like I remembered. Spare, but there were always busy people in here, and counters and counters of food. Of course, we only came in when there were lots of guests and so lots of food."

Tom explained her connection. "Josie helped her dad deliver from the grocery."

"Just tell me where you want this set up." She stopped talking long enough for Annie to shrug.

Then she continued as if she hadn't asked. "I can set it up on the island, buffet style and then we can go into the dining room to eat. Just us, then? I always thought that was the prettiest room in the house, but then I didn't ever get to go upstairs, or into the attic or even into the cellar."

"Oh, my." Tom was helping Josie set out the food, pulling dishes and things from the bags and handing them to her. "I forgot to show you the cellar, and also the attic."

"I have an attic? I always wanted an attic when I was a child. I thought it would be fun to play in one."

"You have an attic," responded Joanne. "I've been up there." She pointed to her husband. "We helped empty some things out of there, but there's still a ton of stuff. We put it all into trunks and wardrobes. Mice, you know."

"I'm learning. I'm told they are destructive."

John spoke as he loaded a plate with casserole, carrots and garlic bread. "You have no idea the havoc they'll create. In a short time, they can turn a house into just shreds if left alone." He stood aside and let his wife fill her plate. "Lots of people have mice and just don't know it. The mice will eat off dirty plates, dropped food, bird seed or whatever. But if people move out, watch out."

Joanne stepped aside to let Tom at the buffet. "Enough of mice, now. We're about to eat."

"Oh, sure, sure. It sure looks good, Josie. I haven't had your China pie for a long time."

The five took their plates into the dining area and sat. Conversation was sparse as the hungry folks started on their meal.

Tom was the first to notice the lull I conversation. "It'll be nice to have this big old place occupied again."

Joanne paused her eating. "So, Annie. Is it just you?"

"Yes. My folks died a few years back. They went together. A tree fell on their car." She focused her eyes on her plate but didn't bring any food to her mouth.

"Oh. I didn't realize. Really. A tree fell on their car? It sounds too fantastic to be true."

John gave her a warning look. "Truth is often stranger than fiction. Some really odd things happen in this old world. Sorry for your loss. So, no siblings, then?"

"No siblings, no boyfriend, which I know will be the next question asked, and no, no girlfriend, which you all want to know. I'm pretty much alone." She finally dragged her eyes up from her plate and looked around the table. Most of the plates were now bare. She swallowed hard, took a sip of her water and continued. "You can tell anyone that asks that I do plan to stay. When Covid hit, I was in finance in New York City."

"New York City? Wow. I thought I always wanted to visit, Broadway, the Macy's Parade. Stuff like that." Joanne pushed back her plate. "Just a visit. Too many people for my taste."

The Topped Toff

"Anyone want dessert? I've brought along a trifle. I didn't know how many would be here."

"Oh, yes. I love your trifle," responded Tom. "Let me help you."

Joanne stood and started gathering plates.

John spoke up when she had gone to the kitchen with a handful. "She means well. She's curious by nature. It's what makes her a great pal in the store."

"No problem. I just am finding the sudden change unnerving."

"And you are a bit shy, too. Josie is not, nor is Joanne."

"I noticed."

Josie reentered the dining area with a large clear bowl of trifle, colorful with berries, chocolate sponge pieces and snow-white whipped cream.

"Wow." Annie couldn't wait to taste the elegant dessert, but she could see it had been prepared for a much larger group of people.

Conversation slacked off again as the luscious confection was eaten.

Tom was the first finished, after two helpings. "As good as I remember. Do you remember the apple one you brought when Mom was so ill?"

"I do. I debated doing that one or this one with berries, but the store had such great berries."

"It's been great getting to know you, but gotta' go." John was pushing back his chair.

"Need help cleaning up?" Joanne also pushed back her chair.

"I'll help." Tom was pushing back his chair, but not standing up.

"Me too." Josie looked at Tom and nodded once. "Go, you two. We'll get it done. Won't take long. Most is throw-away or coming home with me."

"Good. See you then." The couple left quickly.

Tom rubbed his stomach. "That was wonderful. I think I need to come round your place from time to time." He laughed, as it was where he usually ate. He was looking at Josie.

She smiled brilliantly at his comment and Annie got the impression Josie loved to feed him.

≡   ≡   ≡

Chapter 5

Monday morning dawned grey and overcast. The lake was white with foamy wind-whipped water.

She took a moment to wonder where loons and ducks went when the water was like this. Did they stay on land?

She fixed a cup of coffee and sat in the kitchen, her kitchen now. What a change in her life. And she had no one to brag to or share with. The people she knew in the city were workmates rather than friends. Josie, from the inn, was more of a friend. She wondered if Josie had always lived here, done anything before running the inn, and how she had acquired the building. She'd ask sometime.

"Well, off we go." She'd almost expected Tom to pop in, decided she didn't need him, and wanted to explore both the attic and the basement. Almost scared to do so, as that was where all those horror movies were focused on, she felt excitement, too.. "Here goes nothing. Always wanted me an attic."

As she headed for the stairs that went up from the kitchen to the upper floor, she consciously threw her shoulders back. "This kitchen is almost bigger than my apartment." Did she want to keep that precious apartment in New York City, a *pied-a-terre*? Could she afford it? She wasn't going to get the money that went with the estate for six months. Up the stairs she went.

There was a door at the foot of the stairs, one at the top. That's why she hadn't thought of the attic before, as this looked like a closet door. At the top of the stairs, she trepidatiously opened the door.

Louy Castonguay 40

The attic smelled of a light underlayer of dust and something she couldn't identify. She topped the stairs and stepped out onto the floor, a broad board pine floor. She sneezed from the dust and had trouble catching her breath. She had expected cobwebs and saw none.

It was one large room, running the length and breadth of the house. The top of the room was showing some exposed support beams, and above those was a wooden ceiling hiding most of the roof work, but she knew there was little between herself and that roof, as the rough work sloped along the roofline. It would be freezing up here in winter and boiling in summer.

There was a window at each end, and on the lakeside, there were two dormer windows near each other about midway, giving light to the whole of the attic.

The were trunks and wardrobes scattered around. Eager to see what had been left behind by previous generations, she opened the one nearest the top of the stairs. The scent of cedar assaulted. "Ah. That's it, cedar.". She looked around and saw there were four wardrobes, the old-fashioned way of keeping clothes, predating closets. She thought she'd seen some closets in most of the rooms, so maybe they'd been added at some point after the house had been built. When had the house been built. Her grandmother and Great Aunt Kelly Marie had probably been born here, but the house would have been old then. So, that might have been the early fifties. Had Kelly been younger or older than Louise? So many questions.

Someone had alluded that this had been given to someone by a guilty husband, or something. Maybe her great grandparents? She'd have to find out if they'd even lived

The Topped Toff   41

here before Kelly Marie. And did they build the house, or did they buy a house that was already built? That might have put it just after the depression, maybe?

She turned her attention to the wardrobe she'd opened. It was filled with clothes. Colorful silk dresses and dark men's formal clothes. By the style, she thought it was clothes from the flapper era with sequins, rhinestones sheer short sleeves and straight skirts. She pulled out a bright yellow and gold dress with a low low neckline. She looked at a few other items, put them back and closed the door, eager to look at other wardrobes and to see what the trunks held.

She pawed through clothes from different eras, in awe of how, as a little girl, she would have enjoyed playing dress up in these, but wondering at the people who had worn them. So much history. So many lost family stories.

She had exhausted the search of the wardrobes and sat beside a trunk, ready to open it when she spied a suitcase, a large leather suitcase of years gone by. She went to it. It was out of place, not piled with other suitcases she'd spied, but pushed back under and eave, as if to put it out of sight. It had leather security straps binding it, for travel.

She unbuckled the straps, hoping it wasn't locked. When she finally got it opened, it was indeed full. Men's clothes, Tye died shirts, bell bottom jeans, a shag vest, hippie stuff. Things from several generations back. Platform shoes, men's underwear, several button-down shirts, a knit suit, several narrow ties, another pair of shoes, dress black lace ups. Someone had worn both dress clothes and hippie stuff. Who left and left underwear behind? Kelly never married. Her brother died in childhood. If her math held, her grandfather would have been of this age, to do the hippie thing? What had happened in this house?

Annie put all the things back in the suitcase. Maybe some of the locals would know. She kept exploring, opening trunks and trunks. Most were filled with clothes from different eras and all of it smelled of moth balls and lavender. One trunk was full of pictures and picture albums. She put it all back while wondering who the people in the pictures were. Another one was full of papers. School reports, house grocery inventory, bills for house repairs, purchases of one kind or another, all neatly in folders. She found a diary or journal and she kept that out to investigate further. She couldn't tell, at a glance, who had written it. She suspected there were more, further down in the trunk and would come back to this trunk to dig deeper. She put everything else back and moved on.

She stood and looked around at the enormous amount of things she had acquired. It was overwhelming. One more trunk to open. This one was shaped differently. It looked like a seaman's trunk, a traveling locker. It didn't want to open, but she worked at it and finally finagled the lock open, lifted the lid and gasped. It was filled with bones. Why would someone fill a trunk with bones and keep it? Where did the bones come from? Why store them. She didn't dare touch any of them, but just stared. As she did, she realized she could identify some of them. A spine, for sure, still whole. Below the bones on top was something leathery. Maybe this was one of those artificial medical skeletons? Or a favorite dog, or something. As she visually examined the bones, something caught her attention, in the corner, below the spine. It was a skull.

She jumped up but didn't run. She just stared down into the box full of bones. "Human. This is human."

Then she ran for the stairs, her breathing hard, her heart pumping. She held the handrail tight so's not to fall but bolted downstairs, then down into the kitchen. She pulled her cell out of her purse and dialed Tom. Her hands were shaking. She wanted to run back upstairs and look again, to be sure this wasn't a false alarm, that it wasn't a plastic skeleton. But there was hair, teeth, clothes, and the smell.

The phone went to voice mail. Annie sat down. Her knees wouldn't hold her. "Tom, where are you?" Maybe she should dial Joe. She tried, and he also went to voice mail. She looked at her watch. It was noon. Maybe they'd gone to lunch together. Still. She dialed Tom again. No answer.

What to do. She was so shaken she couldn't think. What would she do in the city? Did 911 work out here? O gosh, what sorts of secrets had the family kept?

She took some deep breaths and looked around. An empty house, her house now, an unknown family, and a body put in a locker in an attic. Images from scary movies scrolled through her head as she tried to ground herself. Purposefully, she dialed 911. Oh, gosh, anyone. Contact someone. Anyone.

She reached the Maine State Police Barracks.

Her voice quavered as she spoke. "This is Annie. Annie Carlton. I'm in Abigale. Abigale, Maine. I think I just found a body. In my attic. I just got this house. I'm from New York. New York City."

The operator told her to calm down and take a breath. Annie hadn't her felt panic but took a deep breath.

Louy Castonguay 44

"Are you in any danger, ma'am?"

"It's an old body. I mean, it's been there for a long time."

"Fine. Can you tell me exactly where you are and where the body is?"

"I'm in Abigale. I'm in the Lakeside Dower House. I'm not sure of the exact address. I mean, I can't remember."

She was told again to breathe deep. Someone would come out to her. The woman on the line said to hold the line till someone arrived, not touch anything and be patient, as it could take up to an hour to get someone out to her.

She wanted to hang up and call Tom again. She wanted to run out of the house and drive back to the city and snuggle down in her bed. She didn't think she could ever sleep here again. She'd never seen a dead person. Her parents had been cremated. Those grizzly remains, hidden, could not be unseen.

Who would put a body in a wooden box in an attic?

She stood and holding the wall with one hand to keep upright, and holding her phone in the other, she went out the door. She sat by the lake, watching the wind whip the waves into a white frenzy, feeling the cold wind blow over her, knowing she was getting too cold, afraid to go inside.

She heard wheels on the drive. No motor. An electric vehicle.

A shiver ran down her spine and goosebumps erupted on her arms. She wanted to turn, but her body felt too rigid. She was cold, but petrified to return to the house, too.

Someone spoke from behind her.

The Topped Toff

It took her a moment.

"Here. Oh, dear. You've had a fright. I heard the scanner go off, calling someone out here for a body. Who is it?" Tom, then.

"Uh, uh. It's upstairs."

"You found a body upstairs. We went through those rooms. There was no one in there."

"In the attic." Here teeth were chattering.

Tom took off his suitcoat and put it over her shoulders. "We need to get you inside. It's too cold out here, by the lake." He came around in front of her, where she could see him. "Can you stand?"

"I think so."

"Look at me. You say you found a body in the attic?"

"Yes." As she gazed into his very blue eyes, she started to feel a bit calmer. "Maybe it's just a medical skeleton, or plastic or something. Now I feel stupid."

"Maybe. Come." He held out his hand and helped her stand. "If you don't want to go back in the house just yet, we can sit in the car."

"No. I'm fine," she lied, and stood to follow Tom.

Tom took her by the hand to lead her from the water's edge. She felt the strength and warmth flowing into her from his hand. She smelled his scent on the coat over her shoulders, chasing out that other, the rot from the attic. "I'm fine," she repeated. "Let's go inside. It is cold out here, and now you don't have a coat on." She chuckled at the absurdity.

"You'll be fine. I've got a call out to Joe. He's in court this morning. He'll be out, I'm sure, as soon as he's available."

Tom opened the door for her. They walked down the hall to the kitchen.

Tom looked her in the eyes as they sat. He bounced right up again. "I'll make us a cup of coffee. Or would you prefer tea?"

"I don't have tea. I haven't had time to get groceries. I thought I'd go explore the attic. The cellar will be next. Gosh, this has given me a fright."

"I can only imagine. I'll stay until this resolves itself."

She looked at him, puzzled. "Don't you have a job, or something?"

"I'm sort of self-employed. I do pretty much what I want, I guess." He turned from the stove and smiled at her. "I'll just stay."

"I am so grateful. In the city, I guess I had no one, I was used to doing things on my own, but I never had anything like this happen. I couldn't get you, so I called 911. I mean, it looks like a body. It's been there a while, though."

It took only a few minutes for the coffee to be ready. "I'm putting sugar in. It will help calm the nerves. Steady you some." After he had set two cups on the table, he sat again, and he took hold of the hand she'd set down on the table. "We'll get you through this. Tell me what you did in the city."

In a rambling way, told how she'd gotten an apartment. "This kitchen is almost bigger than a New York City apartment. I feel like I'm in some sort of dream."

The Topped Toff 47

Still holding his hand as an anchor, she recited how she'd always wanted to be in finance, imagining it was something glorious and full of numerical mystery. She related how she'd wanted to delve into those mysteries of numbers, but found that the jobs were more mundane, boring, mostly transferring numbers and making sure they balanced. It would be years and years before she could get the sort of job where she could be in a position to actually analyze what the numbers meant, or maybe she'd have to get a higher degree. She finally admitted that she had found the whole thing boring, not challenging at all. She'd been thinking of making a change for a while. "And here I am. I hadn't imagined this sort of change. And now look."

There was a knock on the door. "State Police."

Tom motioned her to stay and went to let them in. Two Maine State Troopers. Smart in their uniforms, holding navy blue visored hats in hand as they entered the kitchen. "Ma'am.

≡   ≡   ≡

Chapter 6

Tom sat down and looked at the troopers. He took Annie by the hand again.

They looked at him, then Annie. "So, a body, we're told?"

"Yes. I just got here. This house was left to me. I went into the attic this morning to explore. I was opening trunks and wardrobes and such. There was this one wooden chest. It has a skeleton, a person, I think. Maybe it's just a medical skeleton, or plastic."

The trooper noticed the hand holding. "You two are together?"

Annie grimaced and shook her head for no.

Tom immediately pulled his hand away. "No, don't be silly, Jim. She told you she just got here."

"Knowing you, that wouldn't surprise me, but good to know." The trooper smiled at him.

Tom ducked his head at the barb, then looked back at the trooper.

The officer looked at Annie. "With your permission, we'll go up and look. Did you touch anything?"

"No. Well, of course I opened it and then I called. I was freaked out and---" She shook her head in disbelief. "I guess I wasn't sure what to do. "

The second man stepped up. "That's understandable. Can you take us there, or tell us how to get there?"

Tom spoke up. "I'll take you. She's badly shaken. I know my way around this house."

The Topped Toff

"And you are.---?"

"Tom Peters Jr. I've done work on this house forever. I'll take you." He looked at Annie. "A wooden locker, you say?"

"Yes. It's green. Looks military, naval maybe.

Tom opened the kitchen door to the stairs and started up.

"Mind if I sit?" Jim, the lead trooper, was staying with Annie.

"No, please do."

"You say you just got here. How long have you been away?"

"I haven't." When the policeman looked confused, she clarified her statement. "I just got here, as in I've never been here. I didn't even know this place existed until last month. I think that's when I got a letter. I was told I'd inherited it, but thought it was a scam. I'm still not sure." She reached for her cup of coffee but pulled away. "Anyways. Seems I had this great aunt. I mean, not great, but as in great grandmother's sister, sort of great." Annie knew she was rambling, but her adrenaline dump was pushing in on her. "I got here earlier this week, that is, in town, but met with the lawyer and Tom just the day before yesterday. Tom came over and helped me get stuff put back into the rooms. It was all bare. Mice you know."

"That's Tom, for you. Always helping." He smiled in a knowing sort of way, then put on his serious face. "Go on, then. In your own words is fine."

"I hadn't even thought about the attic, that this place would even have an attic and a cellar. My small place in

New York City was tiny, you know? Anyways, when I got the letter telling me I'd inherited, I put it away, thinking it was a scam, and then I'd lost my job due to Covid and was straightening my desk to have something to do, trying to get stuff figured out and found it again, and called and well, here I am." She found her heart was beating wildly and stopped talking. She clamped her lips shut, knowing she'd been spewing words out because of nerves.

"Continue. You're doing fine. You came to Abigale. Did you know Tom before?"

"No. I just met him. Him and Joe. Do you know them?"

"I went to school with them. I'm from Abigale. I've always liked the look of this grand old house. So, you didn't know you had an aunt."

"Great aunt. My mother's aunt. Mom never spoke about where she came from. She died. She and my father died in a car accident. I was living in New York, then. I was in finance and living in the city." Her words ran out and she was overwhelmed at the memory of those sad times after she lost her parents and her feelings of aloneness.

"You are Kelly Marie's great niece, but you have never been here and you didn't know her. You would then have no idea who is in the 'box' upstairs?"

She had no words left with which to answer the trooper, looked down at her hands, wrapped tightly around her cup, took a swig of the lukewarm liquid, looked back up at the trooper. "What happens now?"

Footsteps clattered down the stairs and Tom and the trooper entered.

The Topped Toff

"I've called it in. It's a body, for sure. Forensics will tell us more. It's been there a while, and it was somewhere else before that. It's about half bone and half desiccated flesh. No telling how long it has been there."

"No one but myself has been in here since forever." Tom stood near the stove, then leaned on it. "I've been keeping up the place. Kelly Marie's been gone for, what almost ten years, now, and she had around the clock care for a few years before she died."

"We'll look into that," commented Jim, nodding at Tom. We'll wait here until the forensics and detectives arrive. They'll have some questions for you both. So, Tom, how you been doing?"

"Fine. Fine."

"No more issues with raccoons?" He was smirking as he asked, meaning there was a deeper meaning to the question. He didn't explain.

The four of them stood and sat in the roomy kitchen.

"Hey, guys." Tom finally broke the silence. "Can I get you a cup of coffee? It could be a while for the team to get up from Augusta."

"Sure." Jim nodded.

The other trooper also nodded. "Might as well, I guess." He looked at Annie "Won't find us any fancy Starbuns around here.

"I have to keep telling you," said Jim. "It's Starbucks. As in male deer." He shook his head and chuckled.

Tom chimed in. "Maybe Starbucks as in dollar amounts. For what they charge. Star Sawbucks?" He doled out some coffee into cups. "I'd rather make my own. Tastes better."

"I've had me some of that fancy stuff and I don't like it. All those fancy names for milk in your coffee."

Tom set the cups on the table. "I seem to remember you like yours dark and black and no sugar."

"Yup. I want to taste that coffee, not cow juice." This seemed to be a running comment between the two.

"Me, I like to temper the acid. Just a little. No sugar, but certainly I like a bit of milk or better yet cream. It seems to soften the edge a little."

Jim stayed seated, his hat in his lap as he sipped his coffee and teased his former school mate. "Whatever happened to the Elaine you met a while back."

"Seems her life agenda didn't include dating a backwoods boy from the sticks. Last I heard she was marrying this fancy man from Portland. A right proper businessman with a fancy car."

Dennis was closest to the door and heard something before the others. "I think they are here. That was fast, considering." Both troopers put their hats on their heads and parked their coffee cups in the sink. "I'll take them up. The detectives will get here, too, but you two take it easy. Ma'am, it was nice to meet you. And you too," he said to Tom.

The forensics team came in, a man and a woman, all clad in white jumpsuits and masks and carrying a case each.

"Follow me," said Dennis.

The Topped Toff

"I'll just tag along, and then we'll be gone, soon." Jim went upstairs behind the other three.

"What happens now?" Annie was still a little shaken, but getting more settled.

Tom was toying with his empty cup. "They'll examine the scene, then they'll remove the remains to the state lab. They'll try to determine who it was, where it has been for the time since the person died, all that science stuff. DNA, cause of death, how long ago, you know, just like they do on the television or in movies."

"Movies. That's what this all feels like. Like I'll soon step off the stage and back into my life in New York, wondering how I'm going to survive or what I'll need to do next. Or even if I'll be homeless in another few months."

"I personally am very glad, Miss Annie Carlton, that you finally are here, but I am sorry you got such a shock. I had no idea. I've not been up in the attic for years and years. I mean, I poked my head up a few times, just to check that no raccoons had taken up residence."

"There's a story there." Annie felt herself smile for the first time since finding the body. "You'll have to tell me sometime."

A knock came and Tom broke eye contact. He jumped up. "I'll go."

Joe followed him back into the kitchen. "Gosh, half the state of Maine is out there. What's up.?" He looked from one to the other and waited.

Tom pointed to Annie. "She's going to be a challenge. Here a day and she's found a body."

Louy Castonguay

Joe looked at Tom, then Annie, quizzically.

"In the attic," supplied Annie "It was in a trunk, in the attic. I swear I had nothing to do with it. Not my fault. I just got here." She gave Joe a half smile.

"Got it. I know that. Fresh or old?" Joe was taking it seriously.

"Old, I'd say," volunteered Tom. "I only got a glimpse, but mostly defleshed. A long time gone," he said.

"Good. At least they can't pin anything on you. We can both vouch you have only been in town a few days."

"A week," added Tom. "She snuck in a few days before our meeting. That's been there much, much longer."

Footsteps could be heard in the stairwell. Two troopers emerged.

"Hey, Jim."

"Hey, there Joe. Client of yours? Lawyered up already. Could be trouble?"

They both chuckled at the absurdity.

"She just got here, Jim. Blame this on Kelly Marie, or her sketchy parents. Seems maybe this place was haunted, after all."

"We just got called out. Logging truck through a guard rail. Forensics will keep the place clear until the detectives get here. Sorry for your rough intro into this usually nice town." He tipped his hat at Annie.

The other trooper said nothing but also tipped his hat.

"We'll see ourselves out." And just like that, they were gone.

The Topped Toff

Annie could have fooled herself into thinking nothing untoward was going on, since she could hear nothing from up in the attic. With one exception. She was standing in a strange kitchen with two men who were practically strangers to her, waiting for state detectives to come ask her questions about a body found in a house she now apparently owned.

"Coffee," asked Tom. "I can make a new pot."

"That would be great. I think this will be a long day."

Joe took out his phone. "I'll call Josie and ask her to send us some food, a meal, and maybe some snacks for later. Food always makes things go easier."

"Food always makes things easier," echoed Annie.

"Hey, Josie. Got a situation, out to the house." He walked into the hallway.

Annie could hear him, just not what he was saying.

Tom chuckled mirthlessly. "Well, that will do it. The whole town will know by supper."

"This small-town stuff will take some getting used to. In the city, you didn't even know your neighbor, much less what was going on around you."

"Understood." Tom finished setting up the coffee and sat across from her. "Look, we'll help you get through this, whatever this is."

Tears threatened at the kindness.

"Food is on the way," said Joe as he reentered the kitchen. "Josie is concerned about you." He was looking at Annie, then glanced back at Tom, then back at Annie. "She'll be here in about an hour. I can't stay, and you won't need a lawyer's advice for a while, anyways. Just hang in there." With that, he whirled and left, not even taking the coffee that Tom was even then pouring out.

☰   ☰   ☰

Chapter 7

Annie sat and mindlessly took the cup that Tom handed her. She wrapped her hands around it, feeling the warmth seep into her hands and arms, stabilizing her. She watched the swirls of steam above the cup.

"Need anything else?"

She shook her head 'no' without looking up.

"I'm going to the bathroom. I'll be right back."

She nodded, glad to have a few moments to herself, thinking this had to be the oddest day of her life, in this odd place.

Tom was only gone for a few minutes. "How you doing? Want some sugar in that cup?"

"No. Tom, did you know Kelly Marie? Was she an odd character? Why do you suppose I never knew about her? Why did she leave this house to me? Why not my mother, her niece? And what the heck?" She looked up at Tom, and tears threatened.

He sat across from her, a fresh cup of coffee in front of him. "I don't know. She seemed rather normal for an old lady, when I knew her. I'd heard stories, of course, of the wild things that had gone on here way back. Just gossipy stuff, you know."

"I don't. Tell me."

"Well, here's what I know. Her mother was often here alone with the girls, with Lucien only up a few weeks in summer. Where the money originally came from, no one seems to know. Some say it came from bootlegging during Prohibition. But Lucien was too young for that."

He sipped from his cup and stared past her shoulder, buried in memories but only for a moment. He brought his gaze back to her. "Kelly Marie, Louise and their mother were almost always here, but would go off, from time to time, leaving the house empty. When they were here, they seldom mixed with the locals. That's what I've heard." He toyed with his spoon, investigated his cup as if checking if it was still holding liquid. Not glancing up, he continued. "The girls went to private school, apparently, not local and there would be large parties on weekends, sometimes for a week or more. Beatniks, they were called. Artists, musicians, even a few politicians were spotted here."

"I see." Annie drained her cup and put it gently back on the table. "Go on, then."

"Later, things were very quiet, as Anita aged, at least from what I heard. She finally stayed more and more in her room. Louise, your grandmother, never came, not even for her mother's funeral." Tom drained his own cup. "Are you doing better? "

"Yes. I'm fine. It was a shock, is all."

"Understandable."

"Please, do you know anymore?"

"Well, from what I heard, rumor had it that Kelly Marie visited Louise from time to time." He stopped, a question in his eyes.

"I never knew she existed. Grams died before I was born. So much I don't know."

"It's that way for most of us. We don't know what went on with our parents, much less our grandparents."

Just then, footsteps were heard coming down the stairs. A forensics tech entered the kitchen. "We're done. We've done all we can. The detectives will be in later. We'll take him out with us, of course."

"So, it was male?" Tom stood.

"Yes." The man as removing his white jump suit. "We'll let you know when we know more. Rough guess. He was somewhere else when he died, left for a long time, then bundled into the locker after he'd mummified a bit. I'd say he'd died about fifty or sixty years ago."

"Geez." My mother wasn't even born back then. That would have been, what, the seventies?"

"Somewhere about then. I'd guess that from the few clothes he still has on him. We found nothing else in the attic. We checked to be sure you wouldn't find any other nasty surprises."

"Thank you." Annie hadn't even thought there might be others.

"I'd have someone check the rest of the house for you, if I was you."

"Oh, yes." Annie was rattled.

"Well, almost everything has been unpacked. We did that yesterday." Tom was now standing between the man and Annie, as if shielding her.

A second set of feet came down the stairs. "Set, Seth?"

The first tech laughed at what seemed to be an old joke. "Yes, Seth is set." He turned to his companion. "Let's take him out the front staircase, then."

The two turned and went up the stairs. A few minutes later, Annie heard them on the front staircase, heard the door open and then close, and heard a vehicle leave the driveway. Almost at the same time, she heard another vehicle.

Tom turned and went to the door before the knock came. He was followed back to the kitchen by Josie, and both were carrying a bag.

"Oh, Josie."

"How exciting. A body. I always knew the old gal was up to no good." She set her bag on the wide counter. "I've brought along some supper. Thought maybe you could use a good feed."

Tom put the bag he was carrying beside it. "Is here all right?" he asked Josie.

Josie answered. "Fine. I've brought some of my famous chili. It'll cure most anything and put a bit of fire in your belly, steel you up for anything coming at you."

"I could use a bit of false courage about now."

"I also brought a bit of tequila. Old folks were fond of brandy as a restorative, but I find tequila much more helpful."

Tom was rubbing his hands gleefully. "Oh, great. The good stuff, I hope. I am a bit hungry and love your chili."

Annie watched Josie set out the food. Chili, cornbread, along with disposable dishes, spoons, knives and a quart of tequila. She hadn't felt hunger until the aroma wafted up to her.

The Topped Toff

Over the generous and fiery meal, they spoke of town happenings. Tom and Josie seemed to be vying for the funniest story about town characters.

Josie was telling a long story, between bites, of one of her clients who claimed to be allergic to almost every kind of food, but then asked her for meals that usually included those items. Even the internet wasn't up to giving her recipes that had nothing in them. His wife had an allergy, apparently, to not having anything to eat, was always eating and running her mouth when not chewing.

Tom told a story of a fancy restaurant he'd been to in Portland that served weird foods, including the slime from sea cucumbers, freeze dried hot chocolate bites and more.

Soon, Annie found herself laughing along with them. She drank generously of the tequila to wash down the spicy chili. Even the cornbread had some heat to it. She realized her error when she tried to make a comment about the gentleman who carried his pet chicken in a gunny sack everywhere he went, including a local restaurant. Her words slurred, her tongue thick. "Did the serverrr offerrr to cook it for him?"

They were all laughing, both at her comment and at her impaired speech when they heard a knock.

≡   ≡   ≡

Chapter 8

Tom stood quickly and knocked over his chair. All three laughed aloud again. "I'll get it," he said, as he turned to the door.

Detectives followed him back to the kitchen. "Hey, Josie. And you must be the new owner of this pile. I'm Detective Albert Downs of the Maine State Police." He extended his hand for a handshake and quickly withdrew it, remembering Covid protocol. "This is Detective Andrew Dubbs.

Albert was lean, small built and reminded Annie of a fox. She worked to control a giggle. Andrew was shorter, square, muscley looking, filling his suit jacked amply at the shoulders.

"Good to meet you two," she said. She looked away quickly, feeling like someone caught driving and drinking.

"Hey, there," responded Josie. "Been a while since you two have come to town." She grinned, mischievously. "On official business, anyways."

"Yes, well," responded Andrew, ignoring her jibe.

Again, Annie felt there was something she wasn't aware of. Did everyone in this state know each other?

Tom stepped out of the room and returned with two dining room chairs. "Have a seat, you two. Take a load off."

"We do need to ask questions, if you don't mind," said Detective Downs.

"Go," answered Tom.

The Topped Toff

Annie nodded.

Detective Downs took the lead. He looked over at Josie and then Tom. "Where you two here when the, ah, body was discovered?"

"No."

"No," echoed Josie.

"Great. The questions will all go to---". He pulled out a notebook. "Mrs. Carlton?"

Annie stifled the giggle that started up. "That's Miss." She worked at it and managed to put on a serious face. She wished the bottle of tequila wasn't so prominent on the table and she shrugged. "I just moved here. I just found out that this house is mine. I got the keys from Joe, downtown, just two days ago."

"Please tell us, in your own words, what happened? What do you know? No supposition, just the facts."

A phrase from an old television show her mother loved to watch on reruns flitted through her mind and she almost giggled again. She latched onto the seriousness of the detective's face. "So, I slept here last night for the first time, ever. Yesterday, people came in and helped move stuff from storage into the rest of the house. Tom was here and Josie brought food."

Dubbs flicked a hand. "She does do great food." Catching an annoyed look from his companion, he nodded. "Sorry. Please go on."

The horror of the morning chased away the fuzzies of the tequila. "I always wanted an attic to play in as a child. I never had one. So, this morning, I got up and thought I'd go exploring. It is my house, I guess."

"You guess, or you know?"

"Oh, she knows," responded Tom.

That earned him a severe look from Downs. "Continue. Please."

"Yes. Well, I went up and poked through different trunks and wardrobes. The smell of mothballs and cedar was everywhere. There was this one small wooden chest, off in the corner. When I opened it, there it was. He was. I guess I was told it was a man." She reached for her glass, then withdrew her hand and looked up at the detective. "Anyways, my first reaction was that it was a plastic skeleton, like the Halloween things, but then I thought maybe it was one of those medical dummy thingies like the charts that show, you know, half is showing the muscles of the body with layers peeled back, and the other half shows the bones of the body. I must have looked at it for three of four minutes."

The moment of discovery triggered a shiver. What I had thought was leather around part of it was flesh." She shuddered at the memory, but couldn't help rambling, attempting to convey the gruesomeness of her discovery. "And with the clothes on, well, I can tell you I was shocked. I'm told the other people took him away."

Downs nodded. "That's good. Anything else you can tell us? Any ideas who it might be?"

"I didn't know my great aunt. I didn't even know I had one. It's all a mystery to me."

"Very good." He stood. "We'll be in touch if we have any more questions. And no doubt we will once the coroner has done his work and can give us a better idea of who and when and maybe then we can figure out why. Feel free to call if you need anything from us, or if you think of anything else." He handed her a business card. "We'll just go up and take a quick look around. I hear the person has been removed."

"I'll take you up." Tom stood and the detectives followed him back to the attic.

Annie giggled. Josie also giggled.

"Want a bit more tequila?" Josie put her hand on the bottle.

"I think I've had enough." She giggled after her comment.

"I'll just clean up and then sit for a while with you." Josie stood and started gathering her dishes and packing up the things she'd brought. "You want the rest of that?" she pointed to the bottle on the table."

"No. Better take it." Annie picked it off the table and handed it to her.

"Fine. You'll know where it is if you need it. And you are welcome to come over and sleep tonight if you want."

"No. I think I'll stay here. I'll have to sometime. And it's gone, anyways. Whoever it was." Annie suddenly felt sad about the unknown person in the attic.

"You can come stay at the inn tonight if you want."

"No. I'll stay here." She knew she sounded more confident than she felt.

"Are you sure?"

"Yes." She made eye contact as she thought about it. "Yes.," she repeated, to reinforce the comment. "I'll be fine."

Tom reentered the kitchen. He searched her face. "Are you all right?"

"Yes. I'm fine."

The trio sat at the table for ten minutes, with little said.

Tom broke the silence. "I have to go. Do you mind?" He waited to see her reaction. "You have my number if you need anything." He melted away as Josie made a flurry of packing up her things, then she too turned and left Annie seated at the kitchen table.

Just as Tom and Josie exited, the two detectives entered the kitchen, having come down the main stairway. "All set, now. We'll be in touch." The detectives Al and Andy followed Josie out the door."

"Now what do I do?" Suddenly, the stress of the day, as well as the full meal and the tequila hit her and she felt sleepy. "A nap, I think. Just a nap." She stood and walked out the kitchen. As she approached the main staircase to go upstairs, she saw a twinkle of light and went to the door sidelight and looked out, thinking another vehicle had arrived. The lake was glimmering in bright yellow sunshine.

When she opened the door and stepped out, the fresh air lifted her spirits, and she walked out and went down by the lake. Birds in the trees called to one another. She sat entranced, a long time, until the sun started going down, leaving her in shadow. When she stood, stiff from the cold,

The Topped Toff

she looked at her watch and realized she'd been gazing at the lake for a few hours.

"I get to look at this for as long as I want." She wished Josie had left some of the chili for her. Just before she opened the door, she heard the call of a loon. A minute later, she heard an answering call. Her heart lifted as she entered the house. This would be a good place for her.

Tomorrow, she'd call and get internet and television cable. A new television. Next week, she'd go back to New York and close out her apartment, empty out what she would bring, sell what she didn't. She'd need to rent a truck, maybe. Would Tom or Josie go with her?

The evening soon became nighttime, as she thought about the momentous change in her life. As twilight became night, she thought about the unfortunate person whose bones had been left in the locker upstairs. Who had he been, why was he here? Sleep came slowly but was deep.

Sunshine woke her on Tuesday morning. Again, she heard the cry of the loons on the lake. She heard other birds, too, and the sound of something else. It took her a few minutes to identify a squirrel's chatter in the trees beside the house.

As she dressed for the day, she wondered if her great aunt had fed the birds and squirrels. But she'd been gone for many years, now. What did critters eat when people didn't feed them. She had so much to learn about the place she would now call home

Again, her thoughts were focused on the person put in a box in the attic. Who had it been? How had he died? Would she ever get answers?

After wiling away part of the morning it was time to explore the town's grocery situation. It was time to stock her kitchen. She started a list. And found she needed everything, including spices, salt, pepper, flour, sugar and so much more, but didn't need to get it all at once. As she made her list, she thought someone ought to be putting together kits for such situations as this, a sort of "new home" starter. The list got longer and longer the more she wrote. "Just the basics, to start, kiddo."

She left the house before lunchtime, hoping to find a place to eat. Abigale must have a restaurant of some sort, something besides Josie's.

Before starting the car, she gazed out at the lake for a few minutes. "I wonder if I'll be able to afford a small rowboat," she asked the ether. "Gosh. What a change."

≡   ≡   ≡

Chapter 9

Annie found herself at the door of the Inn. No one answered the locked door. Apparently, Josie was out. Annie knew she should have called. She could call now, but she didn't want to disturb her. She went up Abigale's main street, looking for grocery stores. She saw two stores, Maddie's and Lennie's. The buildings were very small, more sandwich shops with a few groceries. She saw a hardware store. That must be John and Joanne's store and moved on. Soon, she was outside of the small town, on a highway. She had come in from the south end of town. This led north. She drove half an hour before she came to signs for the interstate. She hadn't known there was so much wooded area in the entire nation. She drove another half hour and then the woods gave way to closer houses.

"How can there be these many people and no stores," she asked out loud.

She stopped at a gas station to fill up. It was a convenience store and gas station.

After running her card to pay for the gas, she wondered just how long she could hang out in Abigale before her funds vanished. Would she be able to transfer her unemployment from New York? She'd have to do some homework. She missed having internet. Her phone service had to be changed, too."

After pumping her gas, she entered the convenience store. They served both hot and cold food, had a self-serve coffee bar, soda dispenser, a sandwich board with dozens of sandwiches listed, several types of pizza and pasta, drinks and salads.

Louy Castonguay

The store shelves held many items from potato chips to donuts, baking mixes, fruit, and the coolers were filled to the door with both soft drinks and beer, with one cooler just for dairy. She was tempted to just do a small grocery run here and return home. She was hungry. She'd get several sandwiches and salads and return home. She wanted to be home, but her New York home, with familiar things around her.

"Excuse me. Can you tell me where the nearest grocery store is?"

The clerk was doing prep work, dicing tomatoes and peppers. "Oh, sure. You just go down here, about two miles, get on the interstate. That'll take you into downtown Bangor. Bang a left coming off of exit 182. You'll see the shopping mall on your left. Anything else I can help you with?"

"No, I think that's enough. I think that's what I needed. Thanks." She started for the door and turned back around. "Can I get one of those Hoagies, whatever that is, please."

"Sure. Be just a minute." She wiped her hands and reached the shelf below her. She brought out a sleeve of huge rolls. You want hot or cold? Ham or salami?"

"Cold, please. And ham would be fine." Since she had no idea what the sandwich would hold, she thought ham would be safe. She also didn't want to wait for something to get heated up.

She wandered to the coolers and chose an Arizona iced tea for a drink. When she wandered back to the counter, her sandwich was wrapped and waiting. The clerk again wiped her hands. She gave a total, passed the credit card scanner

The Topped Toff

to Annie, and bagged the sandwich and drink for her. "Have a nice day."

"Thanks. And you, too."

In the car, she pulled up away from the gas pumps, parked and unwrapped her sandwich. It was a Kaiser type roll, stuffed with ham, lettuce, pickles, tomatoes, American cheese and slathered with mayonnaise. She knew she couldn't possibly eat the whole thing. She opened her drink, savored the astringent and smooth taste of the ice-cold tea, ate some more, and before she realized it, the wrapper was empty.

Having finished eating, she drove the car back onto the road and followed directions. She easily found the store in the center of a mall that held many chain stores. Bangor seemed to be a thriving bona fide city.

The grocery store was huge. Using her list, she went up and down each aisle and soon had a cart full. She checked out and headed to the car. She found that getting back on the interstate to go home was more difficult than it had seemed. But every few miles along a seeming main road, were more signs for the interstate. Once back on it, she easily found her way home.

At the house, she hauled her purchases in, setting them on the table in the kitchen. As she put them away the image of what she'd found in the attic was foremost in her mind.

To reassure herself that the area was no longer disgusting, she decided to brave the repulsive upper region and go into it. Slowly, she climbed the stairs to the second floor and then the second set of stairs into the attic. It looked completely safe and not at all menacing. Meandering through the open space, touching many trunks and wardrobes, remembering what she'd seen in them all yesterday, seeing the empty spot in the layers of dust where the wooden locker had been, she fought down panic. She'd been assured by the forensics team that they'd checked everything for any more bodies. Sighing, nodding to herself once, glad of her courage to confront the place that had given her such a scare, she went back downstairs.

Finding herself at the front of the house, she went out and walked to the beach. She'd have to get some chairs here, have a few friends, drinks in hand, just watching the sun set. Friends. So far, that might be Josie, Tom and Joe. She sat for at least thirty minutes, listening to the soft lap of waves on the shore. A speed boat went zooming by, a ways off from shore and was gone. Next year, maybe there'd be a boat, out here. Not a speed boat, just a small one, and a fire ring, and some of those slanted chairs and friends to share it all with. What did the future hold?

Back in the house she called Josie.

All the groceries hadn't been put away and she absorbed herself in filling saltshakers, stacking canned goods, and starting a stew for her supper the old-fashioned way, since the house didn't seem to have a slow cooker or an instapot.

The day was far gone when she finished her chores. Back in the library the boxes of books stared up at her. They all smelled lightly of moth balls. Would the smell ever leave? After opening a window to the cooling evening air, she set about trying to shelve things. Most of the books were classics, but some were intermixed with more modern books, with a few paperbacks thrown in without seeming rhyme or reason.

The Topped Toff

After a few hours, she realized she'd forgotten the stew she'd put in the oven, to avoid the dreaded "stuck bottom" and went to the kitchen. The stew was right on the edge of going dry and smelled heavenly. Had she ever been this hungry or ate this much in the city. Was it the country air?

Her phone rang. just as she was getting a plate from the cupboard. "Yes, Josie. I see you called. Sorry. I left the phone in the kitchen."

Josie gave a small chuckle. "Yes, well, I wanted to ask you out to supper, but it's a little late now. What you doing tomorrow for supper?"

"Oh. I think it was going to be leftover stew. Why?"

"I was going to grill a couple of burgers. I'm not able to wait for this weekend. The Inn will be full up. But do set some time aside for Saturday, won't you? There's always a huge fundraiser at the end of August. It's to raise money to help the vets feed any strays that summer folks leave behind. There's always some. Folks like kittens and pups, mostly kittens, get them, then realize they can't take them back to the city and just leave them on the doorstep."

"Oh. Let me think. I have to check my social calendar." She chuckled. "Right. So, no work, yet. No funds for your charity. No social engagements, as I don't know many folks."

"Oh, sorry. I guess I could have led with the fact that it is a free event, then there's a pie auction. Before the meal, there's a grand *'summer's end'* town gathering, down at the beach, always mid-August, before the lake cools, school shopping starts and all that. Everyone then moves into the town hall for a feast and then the pie auction. Some pies go

Louy Castonguay 74

for a few bucks, some from really great cooks, prized for their special ingredients, like Maisy's Raspberry and mango deep dish go for hundreds."

"I suppose folks think I'm some rich folk from the city, but I've been on unemployment since Covid and that will soon run out, and I don't know if I can swap to the Maine system. I'd love to come. I need to connect with the townspeople. Next weekend?"

"Saturday. People start gathering at the waterfront about two. Some earlier, but about two. Wear your swimsuit. It's a measure of bravery to go into the lake, since usually the water is already starting to get cold. Anyways, tomorrow?"

"Yes. Count me in. And next weekend, too."

"Great. Gotta' go. Seems this weekend I have the family from you know where coming in. They're calling every hour to see what the amenities are, checking on this and that."

"Tomorrow. Can I bring anything?"

"No. All good here. Just you. Dress casual, we'll be outdoors for some of it."

Annie served herself some stew from the pot, broke off a hunk of French bread and ate at the kitchen table. She had never understood the need for a dining room. Her family home had had one and they never used it, almost always eating at the bar in the kitchen, or in front of the television.

After supper and cleaning up, she went back to the library. She opened a box and found papers. She riffled through them and saw appliance warranties, casual correspondence, bills, sales flyers with items circled on them and more. This would probably be the desk contents. She dumped the whole lot, handful by handful, onto the desk. It all had to be sorted out and now seemed a great time. At the bottom of the box were half a dozen ledgers. Amongst the ledgers were several journals. Written across the top was the name Kelly M Weeks. She set them aside. This might be interesting reading later, information on her family. She shuffled through some of the paperwork. One item she saw was a bill for oil. Her eyes popped. She hadn't been in the cellar yet and wondered about the furnace. She'd never had a furnace to think about before. She knew there was one, and that it worked. She'd turned it on a few times as the evenings were already cool. The bill was more than she received in a month. Was the "fund" going to pay the next fuel bill. Would she have to shut the house up for the winter and go back to the city. Tom seemed to know a lot about all the things to do with this house, so she'd ask.

As she took the ledgers with her, and the few journals, to her room for some late evening reading, she again was haunted by the thing she'd found upstairs. She was eager to hear what the coroner would say. Would anyone be able to find out who it had been or how it had ended up in a locker in the attic? What the heck?

☰　　☰　　☰

Chapter 10

As Annie prepped for bed, her emotions were roiling. She was in a strange house, which apparently was hers, no acquaintances that felt close, a distance between her previous acquaintances, and with a whole exceptional and unusual life laid out before her, she felt she didn't even know who she was. Sleep came slowly. She dreamt weird dreams of being dislocated, separated from everything she was familiar with, including her own body parts.

She woke several times, sure she'd heard voices in the house, afraid to breathe. The first time, she got up and checked the house on both floors. All the doors and windows were closed and locked, and she was alone. Coming from the city, she was so accustomed to having people all around, at all times. City street noises penetrated almost all parts of any apartment below the tenth floor. Hallway echoes and, next door neighbors' sounds sometimes migrated through even the thickest walls and always, underneath all of that was the general noise of a large building. In her new home, the almost complete silence was sometimes unnerving. The silence when she woke was unsettling, except for the sense that she'd heard voices. After the third time, she acknowledged that what she thought she was hearing was in her dreams, before she awoke, but it had felt so real.

The morning was full of sunshine. She bounced out of bed. "What a glorious day," she said to the curtains.

She had been planning to go through some of the account books and journals but left them on the nightstand. Time enough for that later. And besides, there were more where

The Topped Toff

these came from. It wasn't like she could get through them all in several hours.

First things first. She fixed breakfast. In this new place, with all the changes, she felt like eating almost all the time. "Enough of that." She kept breakfast to toast and some excellent homestyle raspberry jam. And coffee, which she took out by the lake.

That is where she was when Tom arrived. "Ah, a great day at the Dower House, I see?"

"Yes," she said absently, still a bit distracted by the episodes of last night.

"Give. What's wrong?"

"Did anyone ever say this house was haunted?"

"No. And yes." He flashed a half smile at her, then his eyes crinkled as he gave her a full smile.

"Explain that."

"No, not exactly. But while Kelly Marie was alive, and had hired help in those last few years, there were some that alleged she'd wake up claiming to have heard voices, voices from those that were dead and gone."

"That sounds like a haunting."

"It's presumed it was in her head, since no one else heard them. She was getting less and less in touch with reality."

"I thought I heard voices, like a big party, but when I listened closely, I only heard one frog garumping and the leaves were rattling just a little but other than that, there was nothing, no sound. Nothing."

"The country quiet can fool you. But also, there's the geese. They gather, this time of year, and the geese can sound like a party is going on."

"Geese? Someone around here is raising geese?"

"No, silly. Wild geese. They gather in rafts, do some practice runs, like fly around in circles. Then one day, usually mid-October, they rise up and just keep on going. They leave for the winter."

"Oh." Feeling stupid, Annie went quiet again.

"Look, the reason I stopped by. I heard from Albert Downs. Unofficially. You'll probably get a visit or a call in the next day or so."

"Oh." Annie looked over at Tom. "What did he have to say?"

"He said the body was that of a thirty-five- to forty-five-year-old male. In great physical shape, solid bones, well fed, you know, not a homeless vagabond or anything. The remnants of his clothes seemed to be upper crust. A label suggested off the rack, but expensive, like not tailor-made, but not Wal-Mart, either."

"Geez. Does Walmart sell suits, even?"

"No, but not the point."

Annie was smiling at his seriousness. "Go on."

"So, they thought, at first, maybe he'd fallen partially though the ice, part of him deteriorated, part was preserved and dried out, getting mummified."

"Geez. Can that happen? But then why in a trunk in the attic? Who would put him there? Why not just report to someone that they found a body?"

"Well, their theory went away when they did the full autopsy. Seems there was a small caliber bullet in his heart."

"A bullet. Someone shot him and then threw him in the lake?"

"No. they think he was shot and then put in a freezer. A freezer that didn't work well. His upper half got freeze dried and his lower half rotted away, or some combination like that."

"So, who was he?"

"No one seems to know. They couldn't find any missing persons that matched, from that time, from this area. Records were a bit sketchy, back then, not digitized like now. Do you want him back?"

"Me? Why?" She was stunned by the question.

"Well, someone went to the trouble of preserving his remains. He might be related?"

She shook her head with force. "Absolutely not. I wouldn't know what to do with it. Him. I have no idea who he would be. Maybe someone who worked here?"

"Could be."

"What will they do with --- with him?"

"No idea." He smiled. "Sorry. They'll take DNA and put the whole thing on ice."

She laughed at his pun.

"That's better. But without someone to compare to, well, there's no way to identify him. Probably a pauper's grave."

Annie nodded.

"What Albert said was that it will be an open case, but there won't be much effort put into it. Someone went through the missing person's files, over the last few decades. They figure, from the clothes that he died about 1975 to 1985."

"Well, my mom was born in 1978. So she didn't kill the person. She hadn't met dad until 1999, so it wasn't him either. Gram Louise married in maybe 1970 and she'd left here by then. I never even knew there was a Dower house or an aunt, or anything." She felt like crying in frustration. "Towns folks know more about my family than I do."

Tom felt her mood. "Look, he's gone. All the people who were involved are too, apparently. No need to worry."

"It's just frustrating to me." A loon called out just then and she felt her mood change to one of brave adventure. "Look, I'll be going to find the local unemployment office and find out where I stand with all this. I need something to live on for the next few months."

"I hear you. You can borrow against the inheritance, I think."

She contemplated his suggestion, then shook her head. "Take out a loan? I don't think so. Oh, and might you be interested in coming to the city with me, in the next week or so, to empty out my apartment? I don't have much. I'll leave most of the furniture. Some of it came with the apartment, anyways."

He looked away, watching the water, as if he wasn't going to answer. Then he turned his gaze back to her. "I would be able to do that for you. I would suggest Josie as a better option, but I know the inn will be full for the next few weeks."

"Of course. I don't even know what you do for a living. Do you have a regular handyman job?"

"No, that's my avocation, my happy place. I'm a writer."

"A writer." She was puzzled. The few writers she knew about wrote for newspapers and magazines. "The local?"

"The local? Oh, you mean newspaper. No. I write novels. You probably never saw any of my books unless you like Steampunk."

"Steampunk." She dredged her memory. "That's the people who dress all funny, and there are gears and mechanicals and stuff.? You write about them?

"No, I write novels using that as the theme. Look, I'll bring you one of mine. You'll see."

She checked to see if he was teasing. "I'd like that. I normally read financial books and journals." She looked back at the lake, afraid to look at him as she asked again. "Are you with me on a road trip to the big city?"

"Yes. I need to get there, anyway."

"For?"

"My annual trip to see my publisher. He likes to check to be sure I'm a real person every now and then."

"Good."

"I'll take the Cadillac."

"Oh. You have another car?"

"It's a monster-ish Escalade. I got it cheap from an outlet in Portland that sells government vehicles. You'll like it. It's like being home all the time you're on the road."

"Geez. Full of surprises, aren't you! I was thinking I'd rent a truck."

"Or we could do that. I gotta' get back to town. Things to do, and all that. You'll be all right?"

"Yes. I'll be all right. See you." After Tom left, Annie sat for a short time. She took a deep breath of the country air. "Well, back to the fray." Annie went into the house and opened her laptop. Time to find out where the nearest unemployment office was. She also looked up kitchen supply stores, hardware was probably covered by the local store, and she wanted some towels, washcloths, soap and other Bed and Bath items.

When her research was over, she went on her journey to the mini city of Bangor to get started on her new life.

≡   ≡   ≡

Chapter 11

Driving back into Bangor, she contemplated what she knew. An unknown male had been found hidden away in the attic of the house. Someone who had lived in town, if not the house, had known about the death of that person. Possibly someone related to her had shot a man and then hidden his body.

There had been so many people she didn't know. It wasn't her mother. It could have been hired help. The possibilities swirled in her head.

She was in a small specialty store when her phone rang.

"This is Inspector Downs from the Maine State Police. Am I speaking with Annie Carlton?"

"Yes. Did you learn anything?"

"I'll be blunt. The coroner said he'd been shot, then, put somewhere and part of him rotted, part got dried out as you saw. They'll try a facial reconstruction, using what was left of his face and his bone structure. We calculated that he died between 1970 and 1980. We've been researching and found no missing person matching what we do know."

"So, what now?"

"We'll extract DNA and just keep the results on file. Do you want the body returned?"

"No!! Absolutely not! I never want anything to do with that, that thing, ever. What will happen now?"

"It will be an open John Doe case. There probably won't be any resolution because we just don't have enough information. You said this had been your aunt's house?"

"No, great aunt. She died in 2019. Mom passed in 2020. Her mother passed in 1998." I don't think there's anyone else in the family. But then I didn't know about great aunt Kelly Marie, either."

"Strange. Families are strange." He chuckled. "You should meet my family if you don't believe that. All right. I guess that's all for now. We'll be by to get some DNA from you, just, you know, to be sure it wasn't some relative. We'll be in touch, if we get any more information."

"That's fine. I'm not home now, but will be later, and for the next few days, I think. Just call before coming over."

"Great. Have a good one."

As she wrapped up her shopping and went to Unemployment, she thought about the events of the last week. Strange, then stranger and stranger. She felt she was spiraling into a time warp. Thinking about where she might find out about the goings-on in her house, she contemplated sources of information. As the detective said, most of the folks who'd been around were gone now. Maybe she could find a geriatric person who still had all their marbles in place. Tom or even Joe could help with that. Or maybe Josie knew of someone.

There had been sharp questions at the Employment office about her relocation to Maine, why she had left an apparently lucrative job and moved to a place where employment in her field wasn't going to be possible. The interview went better after they learned about the property she inherited and that she'd been unemployed at the time of the relocation.

Back in Abigale, she stopped in to visit Josie for a minute. She found her in the kitchen.

"Hey, what's up, girl."

"Found out I'll be eligible for unemployment in this grand state."

"Mind if I continue cooking. Got a big family group coming in tomorrow

"I'll watch, if you don't mind. I always found cooking to be fascinating. It's like a science experiment gone wild

"Sometimes they do go wild. Too much baking soda, not enough fat or sugar, over mixing, under mixing, ovens at the wrong temperature."

"Just what I meant. I heard back from the police."

"And?"

"And they don't know who he is and will likely never know. He was shot then freeze dried before going into the attic."

"Geez. Really." Josie turned on the hand mixer and swooshed the contents of the bowl.

Annie waited for the noise to end. "They want a DNA from me to eliminate any relation to me. Beyond that, they have no clue and will just do a John Doe report and put him in a pauper's grave. They figure anyone related to the crime is long gone. They estimate it was in the seventies some time."

"Well. There." Josie put the dough in muffins tins and popped the over-large tray into the oven. She took out a clean bowl and added flour, sugar, melted butter and stirred it by hand.

"What's that going to be?"

"Oh, this is going to be blondies."

"The brownies without chocolate?"

Josie titled her head. "No nuts, either, because of allergies. I hate fussy eaters. You're not, are you?"

"No. Not at all."

The two women chatted a bit longer and Annie returned home.

She prepared a sandwich and a few store-bought cookies and went back out by the lake to eat lunch. She saw some blue jays squawking in a nearby tree, then the ducks swam by. A loon called from across the lake, and another answered from a nearby cove. As she sat, she heard it. The sound from the night before. It was coming from the cove just beyond the spit of land. She stood and made her way over and gasped at the sight of dozens of geese floating around. As they preened, they gabbed with each other. It did sound like a group of people talking. She laughed at her fears of the night before.

Back in the house, she went to the office/library and looked at the books that had been put on the shelves. Thinking of reorganizing the books in some sort of meaningful way, she moved a few, thought about the ledgers and journals waiting for her by her bed and went to get them. She sat at the desk and started leafing through the ledgers first.

The Topped Toff

Most were household accounts. Quickly leafing through, she saw groceries, heating oil, and repairs to an aging house. Large ticket items that caught her eye included a new roof put on in 1950, and new windows in 1965. There was an uptick of groceries about once a month, probably for those crazy parties she'd heard about. Nothing unusual, nothing surprising. She set aside the majority of financial records and moved on to journals. She sorted them. Anita Guay Weeks had the largest pile.

Annie understood journals had been the Facebook posts of their day. Feelings, moods, things happening, both mundane and world shaking. Anita's journals started in 1940. She would have been just coming into her teen years.

Annie read diligently, at first, about school-girl concerns: friends, boys, school events, a prize for spelling, a bad report about math, and boys.

They came to the Dower in 1941, Lucien had stayed two weeks and left for war. She recorded the birth of her boy, Peter. She lamented her isolated barren life, took joy in all the small achievements of her growing boy, feared for her husband, recorded every time he sent a card or letter, sent him a dutiful wife message once a week, recorded what she'd put in the letter, mostly news about the growing son, and then nothing for a few months but a date. Annie skimmed over most of it. Then there were pages of just dates.

When the writing would pick up again, she had written of the miscarriage she'd had just after the war ended and the depression that followed.

Annie quickly flipped through the pages and read of the death of the son Peter in 1945. He fell ill and his fever was high, and he died the next day. Lucien's name often came up in the journal. Anita wrote pages about her sadness.

Sadness was then eclipsed by joy at the mention of a pregnancy and the birth of a girl in 1948.

Annie flipped through pages of baby notes. She found another girl was born in 1954. Again, the journal was filled with dates and no comments for almost a year.

She restarted her writings with the absence of her husband as he 'took care of business' in Boston. Annie saw no mention of what the business was. She read that Lucien seldom came up to the country and refused to allow her to move down to Boston. Further on, there was mention of a suspicion of a mistress.

Annie put the journals down, tears leaking from her eyes for this woman she'd never known about, secluded here in this huge house in this marvelous setting.

She went to the kitchen to prepare supper. She laughed at herself. She'd picked up lots of groceries, but much of it was the sort of thing she'd been fixing back in the city where meals were mostly takeout or frozen prepared microwaveable things. She could go to Josie, maybe, to take a few cooking lessons. She turned away and left the kitchen, not really feeling hungry.

Her only contact with the outside world was currently her phone. She needed to get a computer, a television, and cable for those and wondered if there was already a line out here for them.

Tomorrow, she decided. She went back to the library, looked at the pile of journals and ledgers, moved the pile of read ones off the desk and onto a shelf, pulled up another box of them, shifted it all once more and went to the bookshelves. She chose a book, went to the parlor and started reading a book from the 1960's about a family living in the deep south just after the civil war.

She had to reread some passages, distracted by recent events and her awareness of things she needed to do to adapt.

She also wondered at the woman who was her great grandmother. She was a lonely woman. One who had lost a child while her husband was away at war. What had her great grandfather done in the war? She didn't even know what he had done for a living, in Boston. Was there any way to find out? To distract herself from the mind-boggling questions, she attempted to focus more on her book, and failed.

Time for food.

≡   ≡   ≡

Chapter 12

Pasta. A quick fix. Pasta shells, a can of tuna, some frozen peas and a can of Mushroom soup. Fifteen minutes later, she was having a nice bowl of satisfying pasta. As she ate, she thought about the book she'd been reading. A family saga. She hadn't known about her family, wasn't rooted in it, as those southerners had been and had no generational family traditions. And who the heck had been hidden in the attic. Who had done that? Why hide a body? How had they been able to get away with it?

She didn't feel the police were doing their work. How could she find answers? She hadn't found answers in the journals so far, but there were still many of them to wade through. Newspapers, she thought. In newspapers from the 1970's she might find a listing for a missing person, or something. Maybe she could find something the police were missing.

After supper, she went back out by the lake. It was magical. The geese, the full moon on the almost flat and calm water, the cool night air all combined to make her feel out of herself. After half an hour goosebumps told her it was time to go back in from the cold.

She went to bed hoping to not have the "haunted" sense of last night and was soon asleep. Morning found her feeling fresh and ready to tackle the world.

There were more questions than answers. Whose body had been secreted in the attic? Had he been an intruder? A thief in the night? A stalker? Some unfortunate stranger who befell the tragedy? Who was the culprit that had shot him?

The Topped Toff

She dressed, breakfasted on a toaster pastry and went into town. The town newspaper seemed a likely place to start. The Abigale Gazette office was in a modern small one-story aluminum and glass brick building on the edge of town.

The only person visible in the small office was a woman who was seated at a computer. "Hi, I'm new in town, but I've just--" She wasn't even sure what she wanted, except to scroll through old papers. "Are your archived papers digital?"

The woman looked at Annie and smiled. "Hi. You must be the owner of that monstrosity outside town. Dower something?"

"Yes. Annie Carlton. Pleased to meet you. I want to dig through old newspapers, sort of connect to the past of the town, if I may."

"You want to know about the body that was found in your attic."

Annie felt her gut clench at the memory of the discovery. "Oh, you know about that."

"Yes. Well, it's my business to know about things like that. I'm writing an article about it. 'Stranger's Body Found in Attic Trunk'. Something like that. I'd be interested in your opinion. Who do you think it could be? Who might have done it?"

"I purely don't know. That's why I want to dig through the old newspapers. Try to find someone who might have gone missing."

"Yes. Well. We don't 'have that here. You'll have to go down to the archive building. The town has a place where they put all the old stuff, old deed books and such. There are sometimes students who come in and work at getting it all on computers, but it's tedious and they never stay at it very long."

"Good. Well, and where is this building?"

"It's the old high school. Oh, I forget you don't know the town yet. Go out of here, take a right and then the very next left. You'll see it there on the left. There's usually someone there. Claire will probably be around. She is doing genealogy of the town founders."

"Oh. Maybe she'll be able to help me. Thanks. And no, I can't add anything to your article. The State Police say it will just be an open case, but they have little hope of finding out who it was."

"You think you might?"

"Yes. Or not. It's a mystery, for sure."

"It is that."

Maybe the search would also help her learn why her grandmother left town and never returned. Or maybe she did return and Annie hadn't yet found it recorded in any journal.

The building was a typical 1920's school building. Brick, and cement whorls and flourishes adorning the façade and obvious window reconstruction, making them smaller, using bricks that didn't match the original ones.

The front door was unlocked, and she entered. There was a foyer with doors leading off in three directions. "Hello. Anyone here?"

No answer.

The Topped Toff

She opened the door straight ahead and found a janitorial closet, with the smell of antiseptic, full of large brooms, rag mops and pails and gallon bottles of all colors and a large floor level sink. She closed the door.

Next, she turned to her right. The door opened into a sort of office complex. Her thoughts ricocheted her back to her school years. This would be the school office, with the principal's office set apart within it, and open doors leading off into what looked like a teacher's lounge and a kitchenette. Wetness in the bottom of the sink showed it had had some recent usage, though the offices looked barren. "Anyone here?"

She then turned to the last door off the foyer and found it led to a hallway. She went into the hallway and found four classrooms, doors open, rooms empty. At the end of the hallways, there was an open staircase going up. "Anyone here?"

She thought she heard a voice but was unsure where it might be coming from. "Anyone?" She suddenly felt unsure of her aim in coming here. What did she even think she was looking for, and why did she think she could solve a case the state police didn't think they could, with all their experience at this. Maybe she should quietly leave.

Then, she distinctly heard a voice. "I'm coming."

She stood absolutely still.

A moment later, she saw a tiny little white-haired lady striding towards her. Where had she appeared from?

"Hi. You must be the lady looking for the newspaper archive. I'm Claire. Julie from the paper phoned me to say that you were on the way. Sorry I wasn't at the door to greet you. I'm sort of the unofficial monitor of the building. Welcome." With that, she arrived at the place Annie was standing. "I'll show you where to look. Follow me."

Annie did. Around a corner at the end of the hallway was a stairway down that wasn't visible from the entrance. Annie followed the energetic older lady down the flight of stairs into the building's cellar.

Clair led her to an open fire door. Inside was a dimly lit room full of shelves filled to the brim. "Here we are. So, just so you know. I'll leave you to it, but please, just put everything back right where you took it. It's all sort of organized chaos down here. I can usually put my hand on anything just the way it is. Eventually, this might all be digital. There was an effort made in the nineties to put everything on microfiche, but then digital became more user friendly. So, if you know what you want to find, I might be able to tell you where to look, but I'll warn you that the further back you go, the less available it will be. So do you know?"

Annie looked at the loquacious woman blankly, not sure of what she was asking.

"What do you think you are looking for? What time frame? It must be in newspapers, as it was Julie that sent you."

Annie gave a quick recap of events at her house. "I'm not sure of the exact dates, of course. Officer Down said they thought it was in the seventies, some time. The nearest they could date it, er, him. Ah, from the clothes. That were left. That is what was left of his clothes." With her tongue completely tangled, she stopped talking.

The Topped Toff

"Yes, well, those would be in the pile over there, please, and just don't change the order of how they are stacked. But help yourself. Ignore the dust. You aren't allergic to dust I hope."

"Not that I know of. And thanks."

"I'll be in the next room. Call out if you need anything."

"Thanks. It looks like this could take a while." She was thinking days and days.

"Good." The woman had seemed so friendly, but now her body language suggested something else.

As Annie tried to figure out why the woman had gone cold and hostile, Claire left the room and closed the door.

Annie went to the shelves full of piles of old, yellowed newspapers. Some were tied in bundles, but most were just stacked. At first, she poked at the piles, checking the dates. The first stack was from the early fifties. She changed to another shelf and checked. Eventually she found the system. She saw the progression of newspapers and figured out the layout. That led her to those of the seventies. The sheer amount boggled her brain. How was she supposed to find what she didn't even know what she was looking for in all this paper?

She took down a stack from 1970. She sat at the table and looked through it. It held one newspaper per week. She worked her way through the stack. It was six months of newspapers. It took her an hour. She didn't want to miss anything. She was starting to get an idea of what was going on in the world at the time that her grandmother and her great aunt were still very young. Pageants, spring balls, baseball wins and losses. Local news, mostly.

As her eyes scanned the papers, getting a little faster in her searches as she became familiar with names of the town folks and the ads for businesses with the owners' names. Still a bit unsure of what exactly she hoped to find, she kept at it, even after her stomach rumbled for supper. Finally, two years into the seventies, she had a feel for this town as it would have been back then.

She had run across Dower House name once or twice, that some event was to be held there. Apparently, it was sometimes used for wedding scenes or retirement parties or other gatherings.

It was after six when she stopped, at the end of 1972, put the stack back just where she'd found it, put the chair back under the table and went to the door to leave. It didn't open. She pushed harder, tried to turn the nob a little more, and pushed again. The door was locked. She was locked in. She knocked and called out for Claire. There was no answer. She called out a bit louder. Still no answer. She screamed as loud as she could, wondering if the room was soundproof.

"What the heck?"

She went to her purse and pulled out her phone. She quickly dialed Josie. When there was no dial tone, she realized there was no reception for the phone here in the cellar. Surely Claire hadn't deliberately locked her in here. That couldn't be. Why had she locked the door? Annie's imagination sprouted ideas that maybe the old lady was senile and didn't remember guiding her into this room.

Annie sat back down at the table. Now what. She stood and went back to the door and tried it again thinking maybe it was just stuck. It didn't budge. She examined the

The Topped Toff

door. She knew doorknobs could be taken apart. The screw in faceplate, however, was on the other side.

She went back to the table and sat, trying to think her way out of this room. A cellar room with no doors except the one that was locked, no windows, an empty building, and only one person knew where she'd gone, the newspaper lady. What was her name? In shock, Annie had trouble remembering. Would someone come find her in here, dead and then hide the body, maybe in her own attic?

She held back the tears. Someone would come to find her. Someone would miss her and ask around. Her car was outside. They would find her here. She was convinced of it.

Might as well make the most of her time. She dug out another pile of papers and started looking through 1973 news of the town. It would probably be morning before she was let out of her prison.

At least she had lights.

≡   ≡   ≡

Chapter 13

After an hour, Annie felt a need for the bathroom and was very hungry. She sometimes carried granola bars in her purse, but today, there weren't any. She also was thirsty. Finally, desperate, she picked a corner of the room and used it as a bathroom. She'd clean it up when she had someone free her. There was nothing to do about her hunger and thirst.

She replaced the pile she'd been working on. Exhausted from the emotions roiling through her, she laid her head on her arms on the table. She wanted to cry, but was so angry at Claire and the situation she'd been placed in. She emitted a low growl of frustration. The door was solid and there was no way she could ram her way out. The door plates and hinges were on the outside of the door. Surely, someone would be looking for her and see her car outside and come get her. Josie? Tom? Or even Joe? Claire would come back, wouldn't she? Didn't she remember she'd guided her down her? Had she done it deliberately?

Sometime in her crazed contemplations, she fell asleep, sitting at the table, her head on her crossed arms.

When she awoke, the room was dark and she was not sure of where she was for just a moment, then felt anger well up in her. Someone had been in the building, and they'd turned off the lights. She tried to recall where the light switch might be. She didn't remember seeing one before.

Finally, she stood and felt her way to the door. Running her fingers along the wall around the door, she tried to remember if she'd seen Claire turn on the light. All she remembered was that Claire had opened the door. The light had been on when she'd opened it. Or had it?

The Topped Toff

Annie's brain buzzed with trying to remember. Had the light been on when the door opened? Had Claire reached for a light switch inside or was the switch outside? Had it already been on before the door opened? Maybe it was on an automatic timer.

Finally, she gave up and cautiously made her way, in the dark, to her table and chair and sat. Hungry, anxious, tired, and confused, she felt tears leak out. She had no idea what time it was. It could be the middle of the night or it could be noon of the next day.

Surely, someone would come looking for her.

Her thoughts went to the body that had been found in her attic. Had he been isolated somehow? Had anyone been looking for him, missed him, wondered what had happened to him? Was she here because she'd discovered him?

Exhausted by her worry, she finally lay down on the floor, stretched out on her side and daydreamed her way to freedom. Claire would come and open the door and 'Oh, dear me' her way out of the accidental locking of the door and forgetting that Annie was there.

Her daydreams turned into real dreams when Annie finally fell asleep on the floor, her arm for a pillow.

She dreamed of a man and a woman sitting by the shore outside the Dower House. They were talking and laughing. He attacked the woman suddenly, lunging and taking a kiss. She resisted and he persisted. He pushed her back against the ground.

In her dream, she empowered the woman who was being so vilely used and she pushed the man off and he fell into the water.

When he arose, he was soaking wet and laughing. He said something ribald to the woman, did a pantomime of tipping his hat, and just walked away.

The dreams stayed with her after she awoke. At the first waking moment, she felt one with the woman, aware how it might have felt to be attacked, and the anger rushed through her.

Had this really happened to someone or had her imagination triggered a sense of outrage that had manifested in such a dream?

Annie slowly sat up. She was very hungry but especially thirsty. Having slept on the cold floor, she could feel her body starting to shut down. She thought about what it might feel like to slowly die, here, in this dark and empty room. She felt her way to the table and sat for a few moments, before she remembered her cell phone. It could be used like a flashlight. She took it out. Still no bars, no signal, but at least the room wasn't totally dark. Now she knew the time. It was six o'clock.

She went back to the door, now with a light. Would she be able to find a way out? Would someone come looking for her? Did anyone really care? Did the collective town hold a secret that no one wanted her to find? Was the answer here in these archives? She returned to the table and closed her phone, returning the room to darkness because she didn't want to run her battery down to nothing, since she didn't know how long she'd be here.

The Topped Toff

Time passed. Every now and then, she'd open the phone just to check the time. It was passing very slowly. Bored, drained by her exasperation at being locked in, she put her head down on her arms on the table and slept again.

She woke to the sound of footsteps. Someone walked by the door to her prison. The steps then went the other way. She screamed. "Help! I'm in here! Someone. Anyone. Help." The footsteps went on past. She ran to the door and banged on it. There was no answer. She called again, screaming.

She grabbed the nearest item she could, a book, and banged on the door, louder, this time. She was rewarded with the sound of returning footsteps.

"Help! Please. I'm in here."

"Oh, Annie? Is that you? Wait a minute. I'll find the key." It sounded like Tom, but could have been Joe. Weak with relief, she stepped back. Then, anxiety twisted her gut when she heard steps move away and she stepped back to the door, both hands on it.

In what seemed forever, she heard steps coming back. She heard a key in the doorknob, and the door opened.

She grasped the edge of the door as it swung in and pulled hard, almost losing her balance from the movement of the door, the sudden influx of light and the relief.

Tom caught her before she went down. "Here, I've got you. How long have you been in here? Gosh. Here, sit." He tried to guide her to the chair in the room, but she resisted, pushing against his guiding arm, leaning towards the light. He followed her lead and led her into the hallway.

"How long have you been in here?" he asked again.

Her throat hoarse from lack of water and the recent screaming, she just shook her head. "Not sure," she muttered, more of a whisper than speech.

"Gosh, you're a mess. I was going to the office when I saw your car outside and thought I'd ask you if you wanted to join Joe and I for supper. I know you said you'd be looking over old records and yesterday, Julie told me she'd sent you over here. Let's get you over to a chair. You look ready to fall down." He walked her up the stairs and into the teacher's lounge area at the far end of the hall.

"Water?" she said, hopefully.

"Yes." He reached into the cupboard, took down a cup and filled it with water from the sink. "Here." He watched her drink.

The water was brackish, in-the-pipe tasting, but she savored it as it flowed across her tongue. She drank again, eyes focused on the cup, as if it would vanish. She drank a third great draught, then looked up at Tom. "Thank you. Claire seems to have forgotten I was in there. I spent the night."

"Claire has left town. She told Julie she was going to visit her sister in Portland. The building is usually closed when she's away, so I didn't think to look for you here, at first."

"Left town?" She looked at Tom, took another drink and then wrinkled her brow.

"I went out to your house yesterday, but you weren't there. You talked to Julie the day before yesterday. Did you come right over here?"

"Yes. I did. I've been in here since then."

The Topped Toff

"I'm really glad I saw your car out there."

"Me too."

Tom reached over and refilled her glass. "Seems you've spent two full nights and a full day."

"It was hard to tell. It was dark. I wonder."

He handed her the newly filled glass. "What. You wonder what?".

"Well, I wonder if Claire did it on purpose." Annie wrapped her hand tightly around the glass on the table.

"Why would she do that?"

"Why indeed." He had been standing against the counter and now pushed away and paced across the room and back. He rubbed his brow, a gesture that was becoming familiar to Annie.

"Why would she have it in for me. I mean, if you hadn't come along, been looking for me, I might have died in there. Is Claire senile?"

"No. She's lots of things, but not that. Never that."

"She seemed like such a nice, sweet old lady."

"Claire? No. She's been labeled a busybody, manipulative and mean. Most people in town steer clear of her. She's older than sin and knows everyone's secrets. She also has plenty of her own. She was the prettiest thing when young and men flocked to her, from what I've been told, but she has a bad, sad reputation of wearing them out. She's divorced twice and worn out three other husbands, who died fairly young."

"I didn't know."

Tom chuckled and waved a dismissive hand. "You couldn't. City girl. But in a small town, we all know about each other. If you stay, you'll learn."

"If I stay. You think I might not?"

"I think you might not." He was smiling as he teased her. "City girl. You'll want your fast food, fancy coffee drinks, Broadway shows, museums, and handy grocery stores."

"I can live without." She frowned. "What?" She realized he'd been teasing. "I can live without all that. I can. Besides, there's nothing there for me anymore."

"I find that hard to believe. No boyfriend" He paused. "Or girlfriend? No addiction to the fast life, parties, all that."

"You're a small-town boy. What would you know about that?"

His smile vanished. He looked aways from Annie. "I know what I know. I didn't always live in Abigale." Seeming agitated, he again pushed away from the counter. "Let's get you home, what say?" He reached out a hand to help her up. "Home?"

"Yes. Oh, yes. From now on, if I go down there, I'll let someone know I've gone in."

"They call it the tombs, where old newspapers and ledgers go to die. I'm glad it didn't become your tomb."

"Oh, me too. Home for a shower and some food and coffee, perhaps. And just for your information, I don't do the fancy lattes and espresso and such. Only on extravagant occasions." As they walked to the door, she stopped, tugging onto his arm. "Seriously. Thanks for freeing me. I could have died in there."

The Topped Toff

He looked her in the eye. "Yes. You could have, but you didn't. Let's get you out of here.

"Yes."

He walked her to her car and opened the door for her. After she was seated, he stopped her from closing it. "So, will you come to supper with Joe and I?"

She wondered for a second if these two really handsome men were a couple, decided it didn't matter, thought about the question, decided she could use friends and these two could fit the bill, rethought that and wondered what they wanted from her, stalled her answer for a full minute as she debated the issue with herself, and opted for the 'whatever happens' attitude and nodded yes. "Yes. I'll come to supper with you two. When and where?"

"We've engaged a table at Josie's. She's renown for her Friday table, serving a ship-round roast beef most Fridays, but you have to reserve a table a week in advance."

"Sounds great."

"I don't want to hold you up anymore. I'll talk to Dave, the sheriff."

She looked at him with a question in her eyes.

"About Claire's behavior. We don't want that to happen again."

Still puzzled, she continued to look at him.

"He's her nephew."

"Oh."

"Have a good day. See you at seven at Josie's" He closed her door. He waved to her as she started her car and drove off.

≡ ≡ ≡

Chapter 14

Annie grabbed some crackers and a spoonful of peanut butter on her way to the shower. She felt grungy, and no wonder, if she'd been in there for two nights and a day. After a long shower she put on comfortable jeans and a sweater. The day was sunny and cool. As she came down the stairs, she was torn between eating and going out to the lakeside. Hunger won. Too impatient to cook, she fixed a peanut butter sandwich with a generous amount of jelly. Then she ate another. She craved a third, but reminded herself that supper would be a big deal.

She took a few crackers out to the lakeside and sat and watched the soothing roll of tiny waves breaking against the sandy shore. The sun was almost overhead, and she felt warmed and cosseted by the gentleness of this place. She thought to wonder yet again why her grandmother had left and never returned, as well as why she'd never heard of it, nor of the sister to her grandmother that had stayed and never left.

Her soul and her body finally warmed by the gentle sunshine, she went into the house. She had found nothing at the town archives, due to being in the dark most of the time, but she still had all the ledgers and the journals. Maybe she could find answers in those.

She grabbed up a few of the journals and settled comfortably in the parlor area of the house, a room she hadn't yet spent much time in. She moved a chair by the window and sat with three of Kelly Marie's journals. She placed them from earliest to latest, though there were missing years between them. Kelly Marie was a teen in 1968 and the journal read almost like a story book, the story of a teen trying to fit into a quickly changing society that was becoming more permissive, global, a war raging in southeast Asia, a shift in music and dress. Her mother figured prominently but her father seemed absent most of the time.

"Mom says I'll have to ask Father, but he's never here."

"Dad came home, and they argued again. Why can't she just leave him alone when he's here so he won't go away again."

"I overheard them arguing again last night, though they tried to be quiet about it. Mom was accusing dad of having a mistress in the city. He wouldn't do that. If she wasn't so mean, he'd stay here more."

The lines repeated over and over in different ways. In addition, there were lines repeating about the two women having arguments, too.

Annie read more about the rough relationship between mother and daughter. Kelly Maire only mentioned her sister once. "Louise is coming home for the weekend. Maybe Father will come up, too. I'll be glad to see her. Maybe she can convince Mother to let me go to the prom with Andrew. Mother never lets me go anywhere. She's afraid I'll do drugs and get drunk and all that."

There's a space of several weeks with no posts.

The next post was virulent. "Mother argued with both Father and Louise. She's terrible. I want to go to the city to live with Father. All I'm told by both is that it just isn't possible. I'll be glad when I'm eighteen and can do what I want."

The next journal was from a few years later. Annie decided she needed to try to put the journals in order and read

The Topped Toff 109

them that way, but she didn't want to get up to do it at the moment. The next one started out on a different note.

"Mother is getting more bothersome. She seems to never know where she put anything. I found the jug of milk in the oven yesterday."

There were more of those sorts of posts. Kelly Marie didn't seem to know what was going on. Annie could see a cognition issue with Anita. Maybe severe depression, maybe something else.

As Kelly Maire approached eighteen and her mother's health worsened, Kelly took more freedom. She was dating several men. She had started experimenting with various alcohols. There was a constant diatribe against her mother and a persistent desire to go live with her father. Little was written about Louise except for an occasional comment about having received a letter from her.

The third journal followed the previous one that Annie had read, but she was tired, and her eyes were straining in the fading light. "Enough," she said to the empty room. "Time for supper. Oh, my gosh." Having forgotten she was supposed to go to Josie's for supper with Tom and Joe, she hurried to change out of her shabby jeans and sweater, into a skirt and silk blouse and ran out the door. Soon, she was in the comfortable dining area of the inn.

"Hey, there she is. We were wondering if you'd got locked in a room again." Joe stood and pulled out a chair for her.

Tom nodded as she sat.

Josie entered the room just then, putting a large platter with a roast on the buffet table. "Come and get it, then. It will only last as long as it will last."

Four of the seven other tables had families seated. There was a cacophony of chairs screeching on the floor and the babble of exciting voices.

A woman stopped at the table and greeted Tom, Joe and put a hand on Annie shoulder as she said hello.

It took Annie a moment. "Oh, yes. You and your husband helped me with moving in. Hardware store, right?"

"Joanne. Yes. If you need anything for that old building, we probably have it, as some of our stock is as old as your house."

"I haven't yet gotten that far with it."

"The store belonged to John's dad and his dad before him. That was in the day before the big box stores, you know, and it had to be a full-service store. We have stuff we don't even know what it is."

"Interesting. Really interesting."

Joanne flapped a hand in the direction of the buffet. "We'd better get to the table."

"Yes." The women followed one another to the buffet, where Joanne spoke to someone ahead of them.

Once back at the table with her abundance of food, she saw Joe and Tom had started eating without her.

Tom stopped eating as she sat and waved a fork in her general direction. "Eat up. And you can have seconds, if you finish before everything is gone. But save room for dessert. I hear that she's made a blueberry cobbler."

"Oh, yum." Annie's stomach gurgled as she saw the abundance of food and remembered that not too long ago,

The Topped Toff

she was in danger of starving to death. She followed the lead of the two men at her table and ate the wonderful roast beef, potato strata, coleslaw, peas, and pickles.

There was little talk around the room as everyone seemed to be enjoying the bounteous meal.

Annie had only eaten half her meal when there was a disturbance. She looked up to see what was going on and it took her only a few seconds to process what she was seeing. It seemed to be round two at the buffet. A few minutes later, Tom and Joe also stood.

"Can I bring you anything?" Joe was being gallant.

"Go. No. Gotta save room for dessert." She patted her stomach. "I'll be full. Thanks." She watched as people loaded plates yet again, being pickier, taking smaller portions.

Watching the people move around the room, she observed that everyone knew each other, and the movement now was more cordial, less pressing. She could see that there was some of the roast left, but not much, and the potato dish was all gone, as was the rest, with only a few pickles left in the various pickle dishes. 'Picked clean' was a phrase that occurred to her.

Tom and Joe were seated again, finishing their second round, but now eating more slowly, savoring the second helping.

Joe caught her looking at the room. "Interesting, is it not?" He waved his hand to indicate the people. "It's a great place to meet and greet, get to know neighbors and old friends, too."

"How long has this inn been here?

Joe answered. "I'm not exactly sure. Built just after the turn of the century, I think."

Tom stood and wandered off, stopping to talk with John and Joanne, then someone else Annie had seen at her house on moving in day.

Joe finished his meal and put down his fork. "How exactly did you come to be locked in the vault?"

"Is that what it's called?" Annie was watching Tom effortlessly float through the room, talking with almost everyone, as if he did it on a regular basis. It took her a moment to formulate an answer. She turned to Joe. "I'm not sure, exactly. Claire let me in. I was searching through the archives of newspapers, trying to find anything about missing persons, or someone who had run off with the secretary, or such. Next thing I knew, the room was in darkness. When I went to the door, it was locked." She glanced back at Tom circulating in the room and wished she was that comfortable with people. But then, he'd known most of these folks all his life.

"Well, I'm glad Tom found you. I'd gone out to the house and found you gone, yesterday. I thought you might have left town. Tom mentioned to me that you intended to go back to New York to empty your apartment."

"Yes. Well. I'm looking for someone to go with me to help." She looked at Joe and realized he was thoroughly focused on her.

"I might be able to get away for a few days."

"Tom said he'd go. I thought to ask Josie, but she's busy."

"Good. Please tell me you aren't on a fifth-floor walkup or something?"

The Topped Toff

"No. I'm tenth floor, but not a walk up. There are stairs, but it's elevator all the way."

"Great. Good. It's been a while since Tom and I went on a trip."

"Great. Good," she echoed.

"Next week, then," he said, as Tom returned to their table.

"What have you two been plotting."

Joe responded. "Seems we'll be making a trip to New York."

"Oh, wonderful. We haven't been there together for a while, now."

Just as Annie was wondering if the two were an item, Joe explained the comment. "We went to college in Syracuse at the same time and spent an inordinate time in the city doing museums and such, thinking we'd conquer the world. Tom returned here and was supposed to take over his dad's practice. He had little patience with it, never liked law, had trouble passing the Maine boards, and then his books started selling."

"I wondered how that happened. That he didn't practice law."

"His heart wasn't in it. He made the motions, but then his father died. I had joined a firm with my wife's family, but that went away when she decided she didn't want to be married anymore. Or not married to me, anyways."

"Oh. I see." It answered Annie's question of their possible involvement with each other. Again, her eyes went to Tom, but then she swung her eyes back to Joe, hoping for more clarification.

"Sorry to bore you. You must be used to more excitement than in this small town."

"Actually, I've met more folks since being in town than I would in the city."

"Anyways. Here I am. I wanted to practice law, Tom didn't, so it was a perfect situation. He didn't have to please his father anymore, I took the business, he writes his books, and we've just settled into our hometown. Well, his hometown. I grew up in Bangor but moved here for high school."

Annie then wondered if maybe Tom or Joe had something going on with Josie, since she seemed a part of a threesome with them.

If given a choice, which of the two might she chose for a boyfriend?

≡   ≡   ≡

Chapter 15

People were sitting around visiting, apparently as part of the meals Josie served. Everywhere Annie looked, people were conversing with those at their table or moving around the room to talk with those at other tables.

Tom said softly "Oh, oh."

Josie made a move to get between Annie's table and a woman striding in her direction but was pushed aside.

The tall, blond woman in jeans and silk shirt came right up to Annie's table and faced her. "What did you do with my aunt?" The room went quiet.

"Your aunt." Annie felt her face flush red and she couldn't believe this stranger was attacking her. Her best New York behavior rose to the surface. "Lady, I don't even know who you are. I just got to town."

"I know who you are. Raking up the past, stirring things, trying to cause trouble. But what I want to know is what you did with my Aunt Claire." The woman stood with hands on her hips and a belligerent look on her face.

"Oh. Claire. From the archive building? Lady, I really don't know where she is. And I certainly didn't do anything to her. She was the one who locked me into the vault and left me there. I'm sorry she went missing, but I didn't do it." Annie stood and faced the angry woman. Her shyness dropped away as her own emotions spurred her on. "She showed me to the room, closed the door and locked it, then shut off the light." She put her own hands on her hips. "She left me like that. If Tom hadn't found me, I could have died there."

"My aunt never hurt anyone. She's kind and gentle and you somehow took advantage of that. I know you did something to her and then pretended to lock yourself in."

"Tammy, quiet down." Tom stood and took her by the elbow. "You know she couldn't have locked that door from the inside. It works on a key. From the outside. We set it up that way on purpose." He put his hand around her elbow. "Someone, maybe not Claire, turned that key. We don't know who. We don't know why."

Tammy was still angry. "Well, then where is she? She wouldn't have gone anywhere without telling me. And she certainly had no reason to do such a bold and awful thing." She pulled her elbow from Tom's hand. She glared at Tom, then at Joe, who had come up beside them all, before she stalked off and went out the door.

"Well," said Tom.

"Well, for sure," said Joe.

"Well, well, really for sure. What the heck." Feeling weak-kneed, Annie sat. The two men also sat, and the conversations in the room started up again.

Supper over, excitement quieted, the people started leaving.

One large man in jeans, button down oxford shirt and leather vest made his way over to the table. "Tom, Joe. And I guess you must be Annie, new owner of The Dower?"

"Yes?" Annie folded her hands in her lap to keep herself calm, fearing another confrontation.

"You probably need to come see me at some time."

Annie looked at him quizzically.

Joe gave a small wave of his hand in the man's direction. "Annie, meet Dave Frost. He's our sheriff. We don't have a regular police force, so the county sheriff's office covers us. Dave, Annie Carlton, new owner of The Dower, as you may have heard."

"Yes, I did hear, and what's this I hear about you being locked in the archives? Is that it?"

Near tears, Annie hung her head. "Yes. I was in for a long time. In the dark." She tried to control the small tremors in her hands, locking her shoulders in place.

"And you seem to think Claire locked you in."

She glanced up at the sheriff. "Yes. She was the only one around." She looked back at Tom. "I didn't see her do it."

"Fine. If you come down to the office, I'll take your full statement." He turned to Tom. "You're familiar with the building. Any chance the door accidently closed and locked?"

"No. Oh, no. It was deliberately set up so that couldn't happen. And don't forget that someone shut the light off. That was deliberate."

"Might Claire have forgotten that Miss Annie was in there?" He glanced at Joe and turned his gaze to Tom.

"No. I don't think so."

"Well, now we have a deliberate act coupled with a missing person."

"Yes. A missing person who locked me in a room and shut off the light."

Dave pulled up a chair and sat his six-foot six frame down and leaned in to talk with Annie.

Tom and Joe also sat.

The room was steadily emptying, and Josie came over and pulled up a chair. "Oh good. Some drama. What's up?"

Dave glanced around at the people gathered at the table. "Let me tell you a bit about our good little Samaritan, Claire. She's all sweet, and tiny and generous with time and money. People love her. But she's a real catamount if you cross her." He leaned back in his chair and flashed a smile to those at the table. "Her first husband left her after only five years. He'd turned up at the doctor's office with deep scratches on his face. He refused to tell how he'd gotten them, but it was plain they were fingernail marks."

Tom studied his own fingernails, then glanced up at Annie and smiled. "I remember hearing about her second husband. A small mousy man. He just plain lit out after one year. It was rumored that it was all he could stand of living with her. He never ever got in contact after leaving. He had a sizeable inheritance from his family, and in the end, she got it all, as he was declared dead after seven years. Father didn't want to process the paperwork but had to."

Annie just stared at Tom.

Dave smiled and bobbed his head once. "My uncle investigated the case of his disappearance. There were no signs of foul play, and he was half in love with Claire, himself, I think."

Annie was no longer thinking the intimacy of a small town was a good thing.

The Topped Toff

Josie had been listening and she chuckled. "The man might have been mousy, but he had a roar. I remember people recounting the huge blow-up fights those two had. Usually late in the evening. The next day, Claire would emerge and be just as sweet.

Dave added his two cents worth. "Figures. That's often the pattern of domestic conflict. No one wants anyone to know what is going on inside the walls of their house, but that is especially true if the husband is the one being abused."

Josie shrugged "I'm not sure which was being abused, just that I've heard they had them some real humdinger fights. Well, according to gossip, in any case."

Tom spoke up. "Julie told me that Claire told her she was going to Portland to visit her sister."

Dave put a hand on the table and nodded. "You gotta' love small towns. Gossip is how I get most of my information. I guess I'll have to put some hours in trying to track down Miss Claire. I do wish sometimes some people would come to me first."

"I'll remember that." Annie thought she'd had enough of community for one evening. "Guess I'll go home. It's been a longish day."

"For sure," said Josie. "I'll see you out." She stood and escorted Annie to the door. "Don't mind the boys, and don't mind Tammy. She's got rose colored glasses on about her aunt and everything else. She was like two years before she understood her husband had really left her and divorced her and moved out of state. She idolizes her aunt. Just saying."

"Got it. I'll see you later." Annie hurried to her car. She was eager for the quiet and aloneness of her home. As she drove, she realized she was starting to think of it as home. Her home. She wished her parents could see her, now. Life was sure going to be different than she'd always imagined it would be. No big city, no high finance job, no steady income.

That thought reminded her that she had forgotten to quiz Joe about what funds would be available to her. Time enough tomorrow."

At The Dower House, she went and stood by the lake a few minutes. The night glow from the water made it seem less dark. The loons, called, just one call. A few minutes later, the call came again and there was an answering call from the other side of the lake. Were they mates, calling to each other? Maybe she'd do a bit of research about loons. Where they like geese, mating for life?

Once inside she had an urge to do more journal study, but decided against it. First things first with those, which meant putting the rest of them in order by dates written. She'd get on that first thing tomorrow.

The loons called out once more just after she turned out the lights.

Before getting out of bed in the morning, she realized she'd have to set a firm date to go to New York and terminate her life there, empty her apartment and make Maine her only home. With mixed feelings, she waivered a bit on the idea, then resolved to do it. She could always get another a pied-a-teres, if she missed the city too much. Reviewing what there was about the city to miss, she couldn't think of a single friend that she'd want to keep in touch with, go to a show or museum with, or even just hang out. On further thought, she envisioned herself as this mid-twenty-year-old city-girl, a carbon copy of so many others who spent most of their time at work. How different life was going to be here.

With a toaster pastry for breakfast and coffee she strode to the library, determined to get some order out of the dozens of journals heaped in boxes.

It took her two hours to put them all on a shelf in what she was pretty sure was the order they'd been written in. A few ledgers had snuck in, but she found that most of the existing ledgers were separated out, in a box by themselves. When she glanced at the ledgers, she could make out that they were mostly listing household expenses, and written in a different hand than Kelly Marie's, maybe a housekeeper or assistant.

Before settling down to work at reading the journals for a clue to what had caused a family rupture, Annie headed for town. She needed to meet with Dave, and she wanted to quiz Josie about both Claire and her niece Tammy. She also needed to arrange the trip to New York with Tom.

As she walked to the car, she heard the loons calling again. This morning, they both seemed to be in the middle of the lake. Feeling pulled apart by her New York and Maine bases, she wondered if she'd ever feel centered, as those loons were currently centered on the lake.

≡ ≡ ≡

Chapter 16

A kitchen worker at the inn told Annie that Josie had gone out to the market.

Annie didn't know where Tom lived. She dialed his number and got voice mail.

She drove back and forth and on side streets until she located the sheriff's office. It was another small brick and glass building, looking like a converted small store. There was one civilian car and two patrol cars, a sign that the sheriff might be in.

At a desk facing the door, a stranger in a brown uniform sat, reading a paperback. He looked up when she opened the door. "Can I help you?" He then set his book, face down on the desk.

"Yes. Annie Carlton. I'm looking for Dave."

"Uh, do you have an appointment?"

"No. Do I need one?"

"No. I'm just supposed to ask, I think." He smiled and when he did, his face was transformed into a magnificent movie star grin.

Annie caught her breath.

He looked down at the phone on his desk. "Just a moment. I see he's on the phone. I'll let him know you are here as soon as he's off." He waved at the sidewall near the door, where two padded chairs were placed near each other. "You can have a seat. It usually doesn't take him long. He's not one to talk on the phone much."

She went to the indicated chairs.

The deputy picked up the receiver of the phone on his desk, pushed a button, muttered a phrase that Annie didn't hear and waved at her. "He'll be right out."

Sheriff Dave was coming down the small hall at her before the deputy had finished speaking. "Hi. Glad you came. Come on in."

A bit nervous about being in a police station, she followed the Sheriff.

"I just need you to speak into this recorder and tell me what happened at the archives." He was talking as he went around his desk and sat. "I'll then have it typed up, and maybe you can come in and sign it. You'll have a chance, before signing, to check that we all got it right. Ready?"

"Yes." Knowing it was being recorded made Annie's mouth go dry. Trying to remember the experience made her hands shake a bit and she was glad she was seated. She heard a click as Dave turned on the recorder.

"Just speak normally, like you're talking to me. I'll ask questions, if I don't understand something."

"Right."

"Time 10:20 AM on August 23, 2022. Present in the room are Sheriff David Frost and complainant Annie" He looked at Annie in a quizzical way. When she shrugged, he said "Your last name, Annie?"

"Ah, Annie Carlton. From New York." Embarrassed by having added the place, she looked at her clenched hands in her lap.

"Annie Carlton of New York and The Lakeside Dower House in Abigale. Please, would you tell us what happened at the Archives Building several days ago?"

"Yes. Sure. So, as you already know, ah." Nerves were making this difficult for her and she stopped to think about how to tell someone about the events and yet, leave out the emotions. "As you know, there was a body found in the house that was left to me in my great-aunt's will. No one seems to know who it is. The state police are in charge".

The horrific memory of finding the body had her clench her hands to hide the shake, but she tried to steady her voice as she continued. "They claim they don't know who it was, nor have any way of knowing who it was. They think it will always be unknown and can't find any matching missing persons from that time." She took a deep breath "Anyways, I thought to do a bit of digging, maybe find something about someone who went missing in that time."

She paused again to gather her thoughts. "I went to the archives to dig through old newspapers. I wasn't in there long when the door closed. When I checked, it was locked. From the outside." She paused to gather her thoughts. "Later, sometime later, the light went out." She shivered, reorganized her hands in her lap, looked down at them, then looked back up.

"Go on. You're doing well." Officer Dave smiled and made a 'go on' motion.

That only reminded Annie that she was being recorded. She took another deep breath. "So, it was dark, and the door was locked, and I didn't have water or food and couldn't really read much in the dark. I apparently was in

The Topped Toff

there for about 30 some hours. Tom found me. That's Tom Peters," she aimed her words at the recorder.

"Do you have any idea who might have locked the door."

"No."

"Did you see anyone with Claire at the Archives Building?"

"No. There could have been. I mean, it's a big building. I didn't explore it all." She shrugged and untangled her hands.

"Sheriff David Frost, completing this interview." He reached out and shut off the recorder. "Done. Now we have another problem. Aunt Claire is missing, and you seem to be the last person known to have seen her. We only have your account of how you ended up in the room, locked in." He was smiling as he said it, but it was only lighting up half his face.

"You don't believe me?" Annie felt challenged and didn't know why. "Everything I said is true." She twisted her hands, looked down at them, knotted them together and looked up at the sheriff."

"I didn't say that, but I gotta be honest. I deal in facts. Your facts don't line up unless there was someone else in the building and they locked you in and took Claire off somewhere." He shrugged then bobbed his head. "Look, I want to believe you. I know you didn't lock yourself in. Tom said it takes a key, and from the outside only. We're solid there. We don't have any proof of when you got locked in. It could be some sort of story cooked up between you two." He paused, apparently waiting for an answer.

Annie sat quietly, her hands locked in her lap.

"I just wonder why Claire would want to lock you in a room. And more importantly, why would she then vanish? Her niece said that if she were going out of town, she would have called."

"I heard her say that." Annie could think of nothing else to say.

The sheriff abruptly waved his hand. "We'll sort all this out. Don't you worry. We'll get it figured out. Just be patient with us. We're a small unit and don't have all the resources of them big city cops, but we usually get 'er done." He stood, started to extend his hand for a shake, and dropped his hand. "Thanks for coming in. I'll be in touch if anything turns up." He nodded to her once and sat.

Annie stood and turned to go. "Thanks. I'll let you know if anything---," and she stopped realizing she was echoing what the sheriff had just said, smiled at him and left.

Outside in her car, she googled U-Haul and 'truck rental'. Bangor had a U-Haul. She was also going to need packing tape, plastic bags, maybe some boxes and she needed to continue stocking her pantry and look at televisions and a few other household items, so she headed to Bangor.

In front of the U-Haul rental, she dialed and got Tom, and then Josie. Tom was still available the next week. Josie backed out of the expedition. "Sorry," she said. "I've got a boatload of stuff with a full inn all week."

"Gotcha", she said, using an expression she was learning to use.

Josie laughed at the idiom.

"Later."

The Topped Toff

Estimating she'd take one day to get there, two days to empty the apartment, and one day to drive back, she booked the truck for Wednesday to Sunday.

"That's done," she said to herself, thinking about the sudden swerve of her life's direction. "Soon, it will be bye-bye city. Geez. I wonder what Mom and Dad would think?"

She went shopping, rethought any large purchases, unsure of her next income, and went home.

The call of the loons greeted her as she got out of her car. Rather than lug in groceries, she went to the shoreline and sat. "How in heck could Grandmother leave here and never come back? And why did Kelly Marie leave this to me and not my mother?" She chuckled as she recalled a show she'd watched as a child. "Where in the world is Claire," she asked the emptiness of the lake.

The loons answered with a long wail of "whooo, whoo," responding to each other across the waves.

She'd miss these guys when they flew south. Did they go south? They must leave before the water froze. When was that she wondered. Confused by all the questions with no answers, she stood up and went to bring in the groceries. As her head emerged from the car with her arms full, she heard tires on the gravel drive. Standing a little too quickly, she bumped her head on the car roof and almost dropped the bags.

The sheriff emerged from his squad car. "Oouch. Did that hurt?"

She gave him a wide -eyed stare. "And do you care if it did?"

"Sorry. You seem to have your feathers ruffled. I didn't mean it like that."

"So, what can I do for you?" She meant *'why are you here?'*

"Can I help?"

"Sure. Grab those two bags. I guess I'm going on a road trip. I had to get some snacks and stuff for the trip. I'll be moving my stuff from New York." She was jabbering and stopped when she realized it. She put her head down and led the way into the house. "You can put it there on the table is fine. I'll take care of it. She looked at the table and realized if they sat in the two chairs at the table, they'd not be able to see each other for the four bags of groceries. She turned to him. "So, why'd you come out here?"

"Well, maybe to see you?" he grinned his half grin again.

She realized he was trying to be social and thought maybe he was shy, too. It was something she didn't always think about, other people being shy. "Why don't we go into the library." Once there, she sat behind the desk and offered him a soft easy chair. "Now, glad to see you, but you didn't come out here to socialize."

"No. We found Aunt Claire."

"Good. That's good, isn't it? Is she all right? Where was she?"

"Her car got stuck. She was in an area of no cell coverage. That's all I know just now. She was unharmed, a little foggy about how she got there. Being looked at by the doc."

"So maybe some memory issues? I don't suppose she remembers locking me in? How old is she?"

"I'm not sure, exactly. Maybe mid-seventies."

The Topped Toff

"So, the same age, maybe as Grandmother Louise and a little older than Kelly Marie?"

"Somewhat about that." He grinned and this time his grin was genuine. It transformed his whole person. "I'm glad you've decided to move here. There was a pool on whether you'd stay or go back to your big city. This old house deserves to be used again. None of us wanted developers to storm in and take over. There's been a few nosing around."

"I'll try to make it work. I think this is a beautiful place." She felt a smile cross her face and she bashfully looked at Dave. "The people aren't bad, either, or at least those I've met. Of course, there's the skeleton that was in my attic, and a looney woman who might have locked me in a dark place."

"You do know the greatest horror writer is from just down the road, right?" He nodded when she looked confused. "Steven King."

"Oh. Steven King. I didn't know he was from Maine. I don't read him, but certainly know of him. I do hope I'm not in one of those horror situations."

"You can call me anytime." He dug out a business card.

She felt he might be flirting but wasn't sure.

"I'll keep that in mind. You take care."

☰   ☰   ☰

Chapter 17

After the Sheriff left, Annie put away the groceries and other items she'd bought. As she worked, she thought about her upcoming trip to New York and wondered if Tom would help with the driving. What might he like for road snacks. Maybe she'd bake cookies, and then scolded herself for not having thought of that before shopping. Maybe Josie would make and sell her some. Fruit, apples seemed popular in Maine, would round that out and they could each provide their own drinks. It had taken seven hours to get here, and it would take longer to go, driving a truck. Where would Tom stay in the city? The hospitable thing to do would be to offer him to stay over at the apartment. She had a drop-down sofa bed. She felt idiotic, not knowing his financial situation, shy about asking. Writing books might not be paying very well.

After her purchases were taken care of, she went to the library, opened her laptop and googled Tom Peters. His name showed up, but actually as a lawyer, deceased, so his father. The firm had belonged to his grandfather, had been run by his father and was now run by Joe Johnson. She found no authors by the name of Tom Peters.

Annie stared at the google screen for a long time, trying to figure if there was some way to tag into the history of Abigale without going into the archives building. Then she scrolled her Facebook and Twitter accounts for any news, which was mostly her New York stuff, since she hadn't yet gotten many 'friends' in Abigale. One post caught her eye. It was about genealogy. "Journals were the old timey sort of 'Facebook' posts." She reread it. Journals. She needed to peruse those journals, which were right here, in this room with her.

The Topped Toff

She prepared a sandwich and a cup of coffee and settled to the journals. She surfaced three hours later. She knew more about Kelly Marie and her sister Louise and their mother Anita, but very little about Lucien. The three women seemed to be at the Dower alone most of the time. It appeared money was never an issue.

Annie made notes of any dates she could.

In the early years after Louise left, she was mentioned a few times in the journals. However, somewhere in the very late 1970's, something changed. It bothered Annie, like a loose tooth, or a burgeoning pimple on the nose. Kelly Marie often posted throughout the journals about hosting gatherings, the distinguished people that flocked to them. The names didn't mean much, for the most part, to Annie, but Kelly Marie seemed to think they were important.

In 1978, there was a large gap in the journals, covering some months. The lack of entries came right in the middle of one journal, then resumed as if there were no missing entries, and there was no mention of what had changed, but the whole tone of things was different.

At the end of that time, Kelly Marie seemed to have stopped entertaining and was living alone with Anita. At some point, Anita seemed to have lost her ability to think. Annie couldn't tell if it was dementia, Alzheimer's, or simple old age. They eventually took on live-in help, Sophie, no last name given, until Anita died. Anita died in 2005. Sophie was mentioned a few times after the death of Anita, but Annie couldn't see that she was living there anymore. Kelly apparently lived alone until she needed live in help in her last few years, before she died in 2019. The journal entries grew sparse in her last years.

Annie stretched and left the library. She had covered most of the journals. She'd come back to it later. As she headed to the kitchen to prepare some supper, she heard tires on the gravel of the drive.

A quick rap on the door and before she could get there, the door opened.

"Hey, there." Tom stopped short, surprised to see her in the hallway.

"Hey, there. Don't people knock around here?" What she meant was knock and wait for the door to be opened.

"I knocked." His smile filled her soul.

"Yeah, yeah." She heard the grouch in her voice and shrugged. "I'm about to fix some supper. I only had a quick sandwich at lunch. Interested?"

"Sure. We can plan our trip next week."

"Sure," she repeated. "Let's. I've got a truck signed out for Wednesday and I hope we can wrap it up and get back by Sunday."

"Sounds good. I hear they found Claire."

"Sheriff told me."

"Oh." Tom seemed put off by the news having already reached her. "Dave was here?"

Annie sensed a slight hostility. "Yes. Is that a problem? Should I be aware of something?"

"No, no. Just, well, be careful with Dave. He has a reputation."

"Oh. Heard. Now, let's plan. You can stay at my apartment. I have a fold down you can use."

The Topped Toff

He put his hand up in a stop motion. "I always stay at the Ritz-Carlton."

Annie's eyebrows went up. That was an expensive, ritzy place.

"It's downtown and my agent pays."

Again, Annie was surprised but tried not to show it.

"We have an arrangement. As long as I produce four books a year and visit New York once a year for a sort of show and tell, she'll foot the bill. It's a business expense."

"Oh." Annie busied herself pulling things from the fridge and pantry. "That's fine then. Will two business days be enough for you?"

"I just really need a few hours with her. Then I can help you box and bag up."

"I'd really appreciate the help." She turned and looked at him.

He was toying with the salt and pepper shakers, seeming to have something on his mind. He caught her looking at him. "Will there be much to carry? Furniture and stuff. We can have a company pick it all up and move it. There are companies that do that."

She turned away and spoke as she sliced onions for an onion gravy to go with the steak she was planning. "I need to save money on this. I just don't know if my unemployment checks will start up again."

"I hear you, but I can help with that. There's the maintenance account we can draw on. As a matter of fact, if you give me your key, you wouldn't even need to go. I can hire it done and all your things brought up here."

"Sounds almost tempting." She faced him again, her oniony hands held up by her shoulders. "Are you saying you don't want me to go, that you want to go to the city by yourself?" She'd heard the accusation and tried to soften the words by teasing. "You just don't want to be with me for five days? You think the city isn't big enough for both of us? Well, mister, my show, my choice?" She attempted to smile as she spoke.

He chuckled, but there was no mirth in it. "I didn't say that. Don't take this wrong. I was just afraid you'd go down and remember what the city was like and not come back." He pasted a half grin on his face. It didn't reach his eyes.

"Why is it important to you? And can't you just Facetime your agent or something?"

"It's easier this way." He started toying with the napkin holder on the table. "Why did you ask me to come along?"

"I asked Josie, too."

Tom nodded. "Smells good."

"Steak au poivre, with onion gravy, microwave 'baked' potato and a side salad?"

"Sounds wonderful. Maybe we can take in a show in New York. I'll have to see what's playing."

"I'd like that, I think. A sort of farewell to city life."

While she was fixing the salads, she heard him clicking on the phone. "Anything special? Any requests?"

"No. Anything that's not too, too out there."

"Gotcha'."

Annie heard more clicking as he worked on his phone.

The Topped Toff

"Done. Saturday evening we'll do a show and then supper at this little bistro I know of."

"Got it." She put the salads on the table, plated the potato, finished off the steaks, loaded on the onion gravy and served him, putting down a plate for herself.

"Sure smells great." He looked up, smiling. "I wonder what it will taste like." His grin was wrinkling his whole face.

"Silly. Eat. Before it gets cold."

"Yes, sir. I mean Ma'am."

They ate in silence for a short time.

"Do you recall anything more about the Archives?" He paused with his fork halfway to his mouth while waiting for an answer.

She was mesmerized by the paused fork, watched it for a moment before answering. "No. One minute the door was open, then it closed and later, the light went off. I don't know exactly when." Bashful about admitting it, she looked down at her plate. "I sort of took a nap." She shrugged off the sense of doom. "I'm really thankful you found me. It was awful."

"I'm sure. And you didn't hear anyone else with Claire?"

"No. I didn't. Do you think Claire forgot I was there and just closed up?"

"It does seem she's been having a few memory issues. Her niece won't admit it, though.""

"She seemed completely with it when I was talking with her." She resumed eating, finishing her salad, but toying with her steak. When she looked up, Tom had cleaned his plate.

"Um, that was delicious. Thanks. You ought to get a job with Josie."

"I can do steak and potato and mac and cheese. A few desserts." She looked down at her plate, embarrassed by the small compliment. "I wonder. Claire must be of the same age as Kelly Marie and Lousie. I wonder if she knows anything. I see a gap between December 1977 and April 1978. After that, there didn't seem to be any more parties or visitors from away."

"Is that when she had a falling out with her sister?"

"No. That seems to have happened earlier, like the early seventies. They were teens, and there are lots of posts, went off to finishing school, a sort of pre-college for young woman, but then neither one went on to college. I see notes about parties here on weekends and school breaks. After finishing school, no explanation, but Louise simply isn't mentioned anymore. Just an occasional post that they'd gotten a letter from her."

"Did you ever meet your grandmother Louise?"

"No. She'd died two years before I was born. The strangest thing, though, is that mother never mentioned great aunt Kelly Marie, nor the Dower, or anything about Maine. I wonder if she didn't know where her mother came from."

"Families. Gotta' love them or leave them."

"I wonder if Anita was already starting down the road to dementia in the early 70's. Seems she'd be too young, yet. Maybe she had depression, or some sort of mental illness."

"I'm sure you'll figure it out. But the past is past and you can't do much about it."

"I'd just like to know who that was in the attic, and why was he hidden like that."

Tom shrugged. "It can't matter, after all this time." He put his napkin on the table beside his plate. "Gotta' go. Something I need to get done this evening. I'll meet you here, then, say about five AM Wednesday morning?"

"Yes. That sounds like a plan. It should get us to New York in time for supper. Ugh. I left all sorts of things in the fridge when I went. I just planned to be here for a few days."

"Life happens," he tossed out, as he stood. "Have a great evening. I'll see myself out."

"Gotcha'."

☰   ☰   ☰

Chapter 18

The next day, in her impatience to find answers, Annie thought of looking in the attic once more. She'd gone through all the trunks and wardrobes, but she went back up to search again. Maybe she'd missed something.

After an hour of searching, she came across a chest of drawers she'd seen and quickly checked the last time she was in the attic. She was struck with the contents. Baby clothes. Lots of baby clothes. Many of the items seemed hand made. Crocheted little layettes, with a cap, sweater, and booties. Also, some boughten items. Some of the items were still in packages. Annie sensed a tragedy. Baby items, so someone was expecting a child, and it apparently didn't live long. Annie wondered if it was Louise. Was that why she left Abigale? She'd had Jane before she got married? Did the dates work? Wasn't Gram married for some years before having Annie's mom? One more mystery on top of all the others.

Yet Annie couldn't help but feel that these were all connected. Something happened. These baby clothes came from the 1970's, it seemed. Did they have ultrasound then, to determine the sex of the child before birth? Most of the clothes were neutral yellow and green, but some were pink. A girl child. Why no mention?

Annie fingered a couple of the items, until she came across a little pink dress with unicorns on it. Why did this look familiar? She put it back with the others. Surely, there were lots of baby clothes with unicorns.

After the dresser with baby clothes, she trolled through other pieces of furniture. There was nothing she hadn't

The Topped Toff   139

seen before, and she saw nothing that held a clue to anything.

Downstairs again, she fixed lunch and went out to the lake to eat. She didn't hear or see loons, but a family of ducks came by. The water was so clear, she could see the tiny sets of feet paddling hard to keep up with mom. The chicks were almost as large as their mother. She watched until they'd disappeared around a point and went back to the house.

In the library, she sat and stared at her laptop for some time. Then she typed in Abigale, Maine and waited for something to download. A whole page of options came up. Apparently, the town had a website. Slowly, she scrolled, making a choice in *'history of-'*. The town had been founded by a 'two brothers who were mining for tourmaline and amethyst, found some and set up camp, bringing in hired help, and the town started to grow, incorporated in 1840, twenty years after Maine became a state, separating it from the parent Massachusetts.

Next, Annie googled the family name of Weeks. She found little. No birth announcement, no weddings, no retirements, no organizations headed by Weeks people, only a few reports of social events held out at the Dower. It was as if they weren't part of the community.

Annie scrolled some more, going from one "topic" to another. She found one posting headed "Elaborate Lakeside Home Remodeled by Navy Veteran." The newspaper article had been copied and pasted and was a bit hard to read as the type had pixelated, but Annie struggled to read about her great grandfather Lucien. He was labeled as *'rich'* and it said he was converting the old town poor house into a summer home for his family. The article was dated 1948.

Annie continued perusing articles until her eyes blurred. There was mention of some social events at the Dower House, some personality that came to visit, a fireworks display on the Fourth of July one year, a Christmas Party for the dignitaries of the town for a few years running,

As she scrolled, she learned that the old gem mines were still open to the public. You could go out to them, and for a fee, you could dig through the tailings, or break rock and anything you found was yours. Down that trail, she found half a dozen articles telling of remarkable discoveries: tourmaline, agate, amethyst and citrine. These were names Annie wasn't familiar with, as well as mica and feldspar which were still mined in the area, still drawing people to the town. She wondered if the wealthy Lucien might have been one of the investors and there had been a dispute about those investments.

Annie finally gave up the search. She didn't want to know about a few stellar rocks dug out of the ground, nor even some remarkable visits by long-gone celebrities. Apparently, that was all she'd get from the local news about the town, unremarkable in a state full of small towns.

The baby clothes in the attic haunted her thoughts. Were there birth records she could look up? After her meager supper, she returned to the laptop. She scrolled sites and factoids, went down one vein about Maine history, which she found intriguing, but after half an hour, she pulled back and returned to her search for birth records in the seventies or early eighties.

The Topped Toff

"Eureka," she screamed. She had found a birth certificate on a genealogy site for one Jane Weeks among the thousands of babies born in the area in 1979, in April. The parents were listed as Louise and Edward Smith of New Jersey. The copy of the certificate had "Amended" stamped across the face of it. "What the heck does amended mean?" She shook her head. Who would know? And how come Kelly Marie hadn't written in her journals about the birth of a child to her sister. Annie's mother Jane seemed to have been born here in Maine, after all.

She figured she needed to talk to a senior resident of the town, and there was no one better than Claire, who seemed to have her hand on all the town records. She'd have been a contemporary to Anita and Kelly Marie and Louise. She might know of something that Annie couldn't find, or at least lead her there. But she hated to do it after what had happened. With a sigh, she closed her laptop and went to bed.

The week passed quickly. Joe phoned and told her that he would not be able to make the trip, after all.

Annie purchased half a dozen large cookies and four whoopie pies from Josie for her trip, froze up bottles of water and juice, guessing at Tom's preferences and put in a loaf of bread then went to the city for a variety of items to make sandwiches: small containers of condiment, cold cuts, cheeses and four packets of prepared vegetables. She also bought a few apples and bananas. They could restock the travel foods for the return trip.

Arriving back home, she realized she'd bought way more than she was going to need for the trip down, grasped she'd be there for two days and then they had the trip back, and started packing the shelf stable items into a small collapsable cooler, moved things to a larger cooler she'd found placed in the pantry by the work crew moving her in, and put some things in the fridge and some in the freezer.

The day before her trip, she went to the city, trading her car for a twenty-one-foot truck. It was the largest they'd let her have without a truck license. She knew it would be large enough and the larger truck looked like it would be more comfortable, less squashed in the cab area.

They left for New York at six in the morning on Wednesday. She drove the rig to his place so he could leave his vehicle at his home. Tom was bleary eyed when she arrived, but he was holding two cups of coffee. Her coffee maker, a Keurig K Cup, was still in the city. The house had a large eight cup maker, which she hadn't wanted to use that morning. Heading out to pick up all her worldly possessions acquired in her previous life, she once more pondered how things had changed for her in such a short time. She'd be glad to have her own clothes and jewelry and shoes and coffee maker, too.

Tom was quiet for the first miles. After an hour on the road, he tried the radio, found it didn't bring in many stations and those were all static.

"I didn't think I needed the extra cost of paying for satellite radio," Annie explained.

"Fine. It's fine. I'm fine with no music. Sorry I seem sort of out of it this morning. I was up late, finishing a manuscript so I could bring it in today."

"Do you have many books published?"

"Not very many. Well, more than lots of authors, but not as many as some of the more prolific ones."

"Do you enjoy it?" She caught his glance at her as she was changing lanes.

"I guess. More than being a lawyer, for sure. I think I'll nap. Just shout out if you want me to drive"

"Sure."

Soon, they'd left Maine.

Tom napped the rest of the way to Boston. He startled her when he spoke. "What's the plan? How are you on gas? I'm hungry and could use another coffee."

"Well, the great man awaketh." She flashed a half smile in his direction.

He chuckled. "Thanks for letting me nap. I'll try to be a better traveling companion, now."

He watched her navigate the city. Once they were out the other side, he sighed

Annie exited the interstate at the next traveler's stop. They went into the building, used the facilities and purchased coffee.

Once back at the truck, Annie opened the cooler, handed him a whoopie pie, took one herself and they stopped again at the gas pumps, then they ate and drank while on the road.

"Tell me, who in the town might know something about the past, about the people."

"Well, Claire for sure. My grandfather could have told you anything. Lawyers and mailmen seem to know all the secrets. My mother might know something."

"That's the first time you've mentioned her. Is she still with us?"

"Depends on what you mean. As in here, with us, no. As in still alive, yes. She lives in Phoenix now. With her second husband. She seldom comes to Maine, but I can put you in touch with her. She was a nurse and they get to know lots of stuff, too."

"And they need to keep everything confidential. I found something."

"Oh, do tell."

"There were baby clothes in the attic. Girl baby, I think, and Mother was born here. I found a Maine genealogy site that lists births and deaths. It appears mother was born in Maine, but the certificate reads 'Amended'."

"Hummm! That's peculiar."

"I just don't know what was amended on it. I checked on dates. It was way after her parents were married in 1973."

"Mother might know."

In Connecticut, Annie handed the driver's seat to Tom. He knew the way into the city and Annie found he was a great truck driver. They were soon at her apartment.

"Tell you what. You have no parking here. What say, I take the truck. I can park at the hotel for free."

"Great idea. Just don't forget to come and get me before heading back to Maine," she teased.

The Topped Toff

"Gotcha." He doubled parked to let her out.

"When is your appointment?"

"Noon, tomorrow. I'm planning on leaving the truck and using taxis. I'll bring the truck here on Saturday and we can load it then. That sound all right?"

"Great. I was wondering where it would get parked. I have an allocated parking permit, but the sticker is on my car."

"I'll take care of it for you." He smiled.

Feeling thankful for his thoughtfulness, she got out of the truck and watched him drive off. "Now, to it." She sighed as she turned to the apartment building, elated to be home, yet dejected that this would be her last days here, what she'd thought of as home. Taking a deep breath, she entered the building, thinking of the work ahead of her. Excited at being back in the familiar surroundings, she found she was also eager to return to a place she hadn't known about a mere few weeks ago, a place that apparently her mother had been born in.

Once in the apartment Annie took stock of what needed to get done. The first job she tackled was cleaning out the refrigerator. That would stay here, along with the stove, and she had no use for the apartment sized table and chairs. For dishes and such, she would need the boxes that had stayed in the truck. "Poor Planning," she said to herself. That evening, she sat and made several lists to help her keep on track.

She slept soundly in her little apartment, with familiar things around her and familiar sounds seeping in.

In the morning, she tackled her bedroom. She carefully rolled and folded and bundled clothes and shoes and bedding and towels.

The clothes and cosmetics and the little bit of jewelry she had were bundled, wrapped and went into garbage bags. It didn't take long. She then went out on the landing and put a note on her next-door neighbor's door, saying she was leaving.

Reluctantly, she next contacted the management company to say she was ending her lease. After a bit of back and forth, they said she wouldn't get her security deposit and needed to pay one more month of rent and agreed to let her terminate early.

The electric, cable, internet, and gas companies were on the list. She wanted to box up her desk stuff, but needed a box for that, too. As she packed, she felt sad that a part of her life was closing, a part she had thought she wanted since she'd been a young girl. At the same time, she felt a newness was opening, something she hadn't even thought possible, and she felt excited about going to live in Abigale. She could always backtrack if it turned out not to be to her liking.

As she methodically sorted what she was taking and what would go in the trash and what she would try to pass on to others, she thought about The Dower, and Great Grandfather Lucien who had gifted it to his new bride, Anita. Was it a guilt gift, or a thankful gift? Perhaps she needed to Google him again and see if he had made a name for himself in Boston.

The Topped Toff

At six, as Annie was debating what to order in for supper, there was a knock. It was Tom. He was holding two large white bags which could only be takeout food.

"You hungry? I thought you might be hungry. I hope you like Thai. There's a Thai place just around the corner. It's still hot."

She stood still, in wonder at the delicious smells wafting from the bag. She also smelled alcohol floating off of Tom.

His eyes sparkled and his lips held a half curve of a smile as he chattered, while holding the bag out like a precious offering. "Can I come in? Will you invite me in? I came all this way."

"Oh, sure. Yes." She stepped back. "You've been celebrating?" she said to his back after he had entered.

"Yes. For sure. It's been a great year. I thought I'd share it with you. So, do you like Thai?"

"I like it just fine. Just, here, I'll take things off the table. I'm starved."

At first, the two ate quietly. Annie kept watching Tom to try to gauge how intoxicated he really was.

They both started to talk at the same time. Annie bobbed to Tom. He nodded.

"So, it turns out that I've a contract for my next four books, and they want them all at once for rapid release, so readers can buy them together, or near each other. Turns out readers of Steampunk are voracious. They like big gulps."

"That's interesting." Annie was being cautious. Her limited experience with drunks was the competitiveness bordering on the combativeness some developed.

"It's fun to write." He paused to finish what was on his plate and take more food from the cartons. Before eating, though, he explained. "Think Science Fiction, Sci-Fi, right? Sort of like the old-fashioned stuff, Jules Verne and like that, but modern, too. So, steam, as in before the industrial revolution, when steam was the power driving everything, but punk, as in modern stuff, like cell phones."

"I see folks in all the old-fashion-y clothes but worn weirdly."

"Yes. It's like children got into grandma's attic and had a go at the clothes there, not knowing how it used to be worn."

Annie was thrown back into her discovery in the attic at her great aunt's.

Tom seemed to notice, and after an awkward silence, he said "sorry."

"Let's get cleaned up."

"Ooops. Not quite finished. I had a lot of alcohol with our extended lunch. I find something with lots of noodles sops it up. I'll be fine soon." He quickly cleaned off his plate and stood. "Here, let me clean up. You go off and do whatever you need."

"The kitchen will have to wait until I get the boxes up here. I've got most everything else under control."

"How much of this stuff is coming with us?"

The Topped Toff

"Actually, just the contents of the cupboards. I won't need the furniture. I'll even leave the bed. The next tenant will enjoy that. I'll leave you to it then. Just set the garbage by the door. I'll go drop it down the chute later, or in the morning. I'm going out and see a couple people who'll be home now."

"Got it. I'll just whiz around the room and clean for you." He sat back down. "Or do you want me to come with?"

"No. They're just friends. And maybe a bit of shopping tomorrow, while I'm here."

"I'll be here first thing Saturday. We'll finish the packing, load the truck and then don't forget our date. The show. I got us tickets to 'The Cottage'. It's a sort of comedy set in the flapper era." He forgot about the offer to help clean. "Thanks. I'll see you day after tomorrow, then, with bells on."

After he left, Annie made a few phone calls, but her acquaintances weren't home. She relaxed and watched television for a while, not having had television for a few weeks. Too antsy to go to bed, but too tired to continue the process of packing, she sat later than she'd wanted to

Finally, knowing it would be a huge day for her, her last full day in her place in the city, she went to bed,

≡   ≡   ≡

Chapter 19

After a restless night, dreaming of strangers partying flapper style at her dower house, like The Great Gatsby she'd read in high school, Annie took a shower and got ready for the day. She put on her city clothes, a dress suit and silk blouse and her pearls. By ten, she was on her way.

First on the list was her coffee shop one last time. By noon, she had landed herself in the little sandwich shop near her former office. There she met and greeted former co-workers, Sunny and Vi, who were still employed. After lunch, she made a supper date with a former co-worker. Sandi now worked for a department store, doing inventory. 'It's a job', she'd told Annie.

After a busy day of closing out social ties, Annie returned to her apartment. She wanted to cry when she looked around at the chaos, knowing she was not only changing domiciles, but her entire way of life, from a lifestyle she'd always dreamed of to one she hadn't thought existed.

'The Lakeside Dower House,' she said to herself, as she got up early Saturday, in anticipation of Tom arriving with boxes. She did what little she could without them, and then went out for coffee and a pastry.

She then puttered and waited through the long morning.

At noon he knocked on her door.

"About time."

"Your agitated. I know I should have called. Sorry. I've been busy. We can close this place up and you can sleep in my suite tonight and then you can go get beautified for our night out on the town."

The Topped Toff 151

"And, if I don't want to sleep with you?" She put her hands on her hips and tried to keep the smile from her face.

"I just guess you can sleep here, if you want, but I'd not suggest it. My suite has three bedrooms, and you can have your pick."

She couldn't keep up the charade and giggled. "Of course I'd like to take advantage of your generous offer. And that will help us get on the road earlier tomorrow. I won't have to wonder where you are."

"Oh, and I got us some help, in all my doing." He stepped aside as four burly men came up the hallway. "This way," he said to them. "Just direct them and they'll do the rest of the packing and all of the lifting. And we got a permit to park the truck out front for three hours. We should be able to get this done in that time."

Annie stepped aside and let the five of them into her tiny apartment.

"Lady, just tell us what goes and what stays. Appliances first?"

"No. they stay. Also, the furniture, including the bed and dresser will stay. I need to pack up the dishes and other kitchen stuff."

"Andy here will help with that. He's real careful." Andy stepped out from behind another man. He was the largest of them.

"Me, I'll go get the trolley and the boxes out of the truck. We brought our own trolley, because I was told this truck didn't come with one. Must be a country truck. The city ones all have four wheeled trolleys. Be right back."

Andy was already taking dishes out of the cupboard and stacking them on the table. "You've almost nothing here, especially if the appliances aren't going. We'll have this done in no time."

Annie felt like a stranger in her own apartment as the other two men started bringing bags out of the bedroom to the front door.

In two hours and fifteen minutes, all of Annie's things were out of the apartment and in the truck.

The leader addressed Tom, who was sitting at the kitchen table. "Hey there boss, anything else I can help you with?"

"Naw. This went well. I appreciate it."

"And we appreciate the theatre tickets. And we love your books. Well, Andy and I do. The others are more into Westerns."

"Thanks again."

Annie, still reeling from the speed of the move, found her voice. "Thanks bunches. Can I tip you?"

"Tom took really good care of us. You have a good life. I'm thinking of getting out of the city, too. The old lady wants a yard for the kids. They are just starting to walk, you know."

Andy punched his arm and looked at Annie. "He had three, all at once. I hadn't realized you could bunch them up like that."

The men left and Tom then took Annie by the elbow. "Time for you to go get pretty."

The Topped Toff 153

She looked at him, pulling her arm from his and standing back.

He caught her resentment at his comment and amended it. "I have an appointment for you. And they'll have a dress for you too. I'll drop you off and go park the truck and then take a cab and come grab you."

"You certainly have taken over the control of this trip." Her resentment at his highhandedness was apparent in her voice.

Tom ignored her irritation. "We'll have a quick bite to eat and then have supper after the show, in proper New York style."

"Proper New York style. The high life. You sure you can afford all this? Or is it coming out of '*my endowment*'?"

"Not. My own money. A gift to you."

"And how do you even know how to set up an appointment for a lady at a salon? I lived in the city for a lot of years but never did any of this, the salon, the Broadway show, evening out, not any of it."

"My pleasure!" His eyes glowed as he stood quietly by the door. After a few moments, he waved his hand towards the door. "Now, can we go?"

Annie nodded, and head down in remorse at her petulance, she followed him to the elevators.

She had a manicure, hair styling and an expert make up. She didn't recognize herself in the mirror. After the personal care, they took her to a dressing room full of gowns, all sizes, styles and colors.

"These are fashion week discards. We have dibs on them." The fashion consultant went to a rack of sparkly bright dresses. She pawed through half a dozen. "Oh, yes. Here. I think this might suit." She had pulled a gorgeous light orange chiffon dress. "I also have this in yellow, but it's a tad bright for your coloring. I do have something in mint green, but it's the wrong style for you."

"Let me try this on." The dress fit perfectly. It was floaty and delicate and less provocative than some she'd seen. "Perfect," she finally announced.

"Good. I assume you'll wear it. We'll box up your old clothes for you. Now, shoes? What's your size?"

With the addition of a small brown brocade jacket and shoes the same tone as the jacket, Annie was dressed for the evening. She was wondering how to pay for all this when Tom showed up again. He was led into the room she was in. "Wonderful. Let's light up the last night you'll have in New York for a while." He led her right out of the store as if they owned it, with no questions about payment. Apparently, Tom had taken care of it.

"I'll owe you forever for all this. This dress alone must have cost a fortune."

"Oh, they just source them from a designer's school for a pittance. It wasn't much."

Over a light meal at a small teashop, Annie broached the topic closest to her mind. "I need to do research on Lucien. A lot of things seem to start and end with him. He died before I was born. Anita died like fifteen years after that. I want to know why he lived in the city and she lived in the country. The journals seem to indicate that she had a

The Topped Toff 155

temper and was often harassing him when he came to Maine. Kelly Marie writes repeatedly that she wished her mother was less argumentative and then maybe her dad would come more often."

"I already did that. I investigated this background. He worked for the Hancock Insurance group. I reached out to a friend. Well, a friend of a friend. Lucien worked before her time. But he had a reputation as a man with a sort of secretive job. The rumble is that he was an investigator, looking for insurance frauds and the like. She's going to dig a little more and get that nailed down."

"Anita seldom left Abigale!" Annie thought maybe she'd got it wrong. "Right?"

Tom nodded.

"I saw a decrease of his visits in the journals after 1970. The girls would have been teens."

After the meal was over, they left the restaurant with no bill or payment. Tom seemed to just walk in and out of places with no worry.

He flagged down a cab and they again were moving through the city. "The story goes that the 'girls' loved to party, including Anita."

Annie took a moment to answer, as she was trying to take in all the sites and sounds she was leaving behind, "That all changed about the spring of 1979. There were seldom visitors to the Dower, after that. That was the year my mother was born, though there's no indication at all that Grandmother Louise had returned. Yet mother was born in Abigale."

"A true mystery. Broadway will be jammed up. I hope you brought your walking shoes."

"Always in New York." She patted her oversized purse.

The show was everything Annie hoped for. The cast had been well chosen. It was a hilarious but salacious romantic comedy staged in the 1920's., that had them laughing all through the show.

Supper after at a small bistro was a wonderful way to wind down the evening. They sat in a small alcove and the bustle of the city dropped away. Annie might have thought herself in Abigale, except no one, not even Josie, cooked meals like the one she ate.

Annie was a bit nervous after Tom's previous inebriation, but he showed no signs of overindulgence. They drank a bottle of wine between them, over several hours, but he refused a second one when offered.

Back at the apartment, he showed her to a bedroom, which had a private bath, stepped back and closed her door. "See you in the morning, then," he said through the closed door.

"Good night."

As she prepared for bed, Annie felt as if she'd stepped into an alternate reality. First the Dower, now this extraordinary night on the town, the way she expected a fabulously rich New Yorker could do it. She'd remember this all her life. What a close out for her time here.

Her thoughts then turned to Anita, stranded, or carefully located in the countryside and Lucien, apparently a force to be reckoned with in Boston. Why had they married and why had they stayed married. Two daughters, with six years between them. One stayed, one moved away, seemingly

The Topped Toff 157

never to return, and yet, she'd gone there to have her baby. That was the thought that chased around her brain as she went to sleep.

The morning dawned bright and sunny, a great day to travel, thought Annie, as she looked out upon the busy city below.

A rap at the bedroom door brought her to the new situation, hobnobbing with the rich. "Enter." The word sounded high-toned to her.

"You're up. Good. How are you this fine morning. He didn't wait for a reply. "I ordered us a huge breakfast. We can take some of it with us for road food. And did you sleep well?"

"Thanks for the grand evening. I so enjoyed myself, but, actually, no. I didn't sleep well. The unanswered questions haunt me."

"Want to fill me in?" He turned. "I made us some coffee.

Annie followed him to the kitchen area."Why did Kelly Marie not mention grandmother's visit to have her baby here? Why did things change so drastically around that time? And who the heck was secreted in the attic?"

"I think we may never learn those things. But we certainly won't learn them here."

There was a knock on the door just then.

"Ah, that would be breakfast. Got your running shoes on? We'll make a break for it after we eat. Sneak out on the bill?"

Annie laughed aloud. She was pretty sure they weren't sneaking out, as he'd told her the room was paid for by his agent. As she ate a breakfast of eggs benedict and fruit cup she wondered just how much he was making on those books he was writing. Steampunk. She knew nothing about it. She'd take time to research it when she got home.

"How'd your meeting go? I haven't had a chance to ask."

"I'll tell you about it after we make our get-away." He laughed for a moment then wrapped the blueberry muffins in napkins. "For later," he said.

≡ ≡ ≡

Chapter 20

Tom took the first leg of the drive, leaving the city. Annie could tell he was familiar with New York and effortlessly freed them from the inner-city labyrinth.

Though busy, traffic flowed more smoothly beyond the city limits. Tense in the hectic mayhem she relaxed once on the interstate, with a sense of accomplishment at closing out her apartment, she was finally able to breathe freely. "All right. Give. How'd your meeting go?"

"Fine. It's always fine. As long as I'm producing. I do about one book a month and the fans eat it right up. It is popular, but my agent is suggesting I might want to start another line of books under a different pen name to diversify. It seems steampunk is declining in popularity. At least it is in her opinion."

"What is your pen name?" She held her breath. She didn't think it was a secret, just that she didn't know it.

"I'll tell you. But you must keep it quiet. Most folks in town think I'm living off an inheritance."

"Oh."

"Promise?"

"Yes." She waited.

"Peter Josephs."

"You used your best friend's name as your pen name?"

"Well, the choice was spur of the moment, but I think it's brilliant."

"Yes."

"What is your favorite thing to read?"

"Business."

"No, I mean for relaxation. Not work."

"All my life *has* been work. All of it.". It had all just gone away. She felt on the edge of tears. "I'll have to take on something else, I guess. Maybe some Steampunk."

Tom laughed aloud. "You are welcome. I'll bring over some. I know a really good author in that field."

Annie chuckled.

As they headed north on I-95, Annie thought about the mysteries she was going back to. "What if? What if we are asking the wrong questions? In business, and finances, there's this mantra. If something seems right but doesn't make sense it isn't right. What if we are asking the wrong questions?"

"So, we've been asking who was in the attic. We've been asking why there's no mention anywhere that your grandmother did come back to have your mother here."

"That's right. Everything changed for the family about then. Maybe that's the starting point. It is also about the time that man died, they think. Why is the birth certificate amended? What does that mean?"

"Joe would know." He glanced quickly at her. "About the amended thing."

"Aren't you a lawyer, too?"

"Well, actually, I did graduate but never passed the bar, and there are different types of lawyers. I'm more into business, corporate, than into the family stuff. He's more into wills, family trusts, custody, divorces, stuff like that."

"Can you call him?"

"Now?"

"Are you doing anything else at the moment?"

"Like navigating the New York freeway with six lanes of traffic and in a truck?"

"Tell me his number and I'll call."

"He won't pick up if he doesn't recognize your number." He slapped the wheel once. "All right. I'm not supposed to use the phone while driving but take my phone. His number is on speed dial under AJ."

"AJ. I thought his name was Joe?"

"The A puts his name first on the list."

Annie took the phone and dialed AJ.

"Hey, Tom. You back yet?"

"This isn't Tom, it's Annie. But he's right here beside me. We are just leaving New York State."

There was a pause. "Speak, Annie. I'm sort of in a rush."

"What does it mean when a birth certificate reads 'amended'?"

"That usually means that there's been an adoption. It will put the adopters name in place of the birth mother. Usually used only for those adoptions done at birth. Anything else I can help with?"

"No. That will do. Thanks. See you soon." She handed the phone back to Tom who put it back in his shirt pocket. "Holy heck. Adoption."

"Adoption. Amended means adopted?"

"My grandmother apparently adopted my mother. That would explain a lot. It would explain why there was only one child. She didn't give birth to her. Who is my real grandmother?" Her whole world had just slipped out from under her. She'd just left behind her real life in New York, and now stumbled into an alternate universe. She no longer had a job, and if Tom was to be believed, she wouldn't ever need one. And someone had died, and his body left in the attic of a house in a town she'd never heard of until a few weeks ago. But most shockingly, her mother was adopted

"To quote you, we may have been asking the wrong questions."

"Wise Guy. But what are the right questions? Heck.. How am I supposed to know anything! I'm not even who I thought I was!"

Tom didn't answer for a moment. "We know someone was shot and killed. A bullet to the heart, apparently. Unless he was shot '*after*' he was dead, that's the cause of death. We can't find anyone who went missing about that time, so someone from away. What else? Maybe he died somewhere else, like Boston, and brought there?"

"And there's an unwanted baby, apparently, who was adopted by my grandmother."

"Who was the mother?"

"Could it have been Kelly Marie? I mean, I keep hearing about wild parties and lots of visitors. What if one of them got out of hand, resulting in a pregnancy?"

"It was the seventies. A time reputed for being wild."

"If Kelly Marie is my natural grandmother, that would make sense about why she left the property to me. But how come I never heard of her, or Abigale, or the adoption. It wasn't the dark ages."

Tom was busy shifting lanes to get out from behind a large truck and was slow to answer. "Granted."

"Can I find out who was on the original birth certificate?"

He shook his head. "If it was a closed adoption, maybe never."

"Joe should be able to tell us, shouldn't he. It might be in the files in the office? Wasn't that the only law office in town? They would probably have handled the adoption?"

"I doubt he'll be able to. Much of that information gets swallowed up in time. And all adoptions used to be closed, meaning the information gets locked up."

"Well, I guess you'll just have to waltz in there and go through the files yourself, then?"

"I can't. I could be sent to jail for theft."

"But they were your grandfather's and then your father's things."

"It goes with business, not the family. Take it from me. I can't get that information for you. You'll have to get it some other way."

"Who might have the skinny on what was going on back then?"

"Almost fifty years ago. Someone in their seventies, maybe? Claire might know. Julie at the newspaper knows about what's going on now, but she's too young for that."

I guess I need to go talk with Claire. Even if she did lock me in last time. Will you come with me?" Annie's shyness made her reluctant to ask, and hesitant to approach Claire again.

"I'd be delighted to escort you to see Claire, and make sure you don't get locked in again."

As they drove through Connecticut, Tom told her about his author career, landing an agent, switching agents, finding his niche with Steampunk, and a few of the plots of his first books. "They were pretty awful. But I studied and it got better. I got better. I can tell a cohesive story, now. And readers of Steampunk are whales. They devour books."

"So, you just keep writing. It's lucrative?"

Tom hesitated, then decided to answer. "Yes. Very lucrative. I'm living just exactly how I'd like to."

After a rest stop, Annie took over the driving. As she drove, she spoke of her childhood dream of being in finance, finally achieving that dream, only to learn she was a glorified scribe, working ten- and twelve-hour days just to stay on an even keel. She described her parents, and how they'd died, together, in a car accident when she was twenty. She'd thrown herself into more work and all she'd gotten was more work.

The Topped Toff

Along the Massachusetts Turnpike, Tom told of his idyllic childhood, with Joe and Dave and others as classmates. He'd been expected to go off and become a lawyer and come back to Abigail and take over the practice. He'd wanted to write, Joe had wanted to be a lawyer, but struggled both financially and academically. Tom helped him study and wrote a few books to earn extra cash to cover life expenses for him. In turn, the work to keep Joe in school helped Tom graduate, too.

"My dad's law business was passed down to me, but my focus had been on the wrong things to do family law. That gave a prefect reason to take on Joe as an associate. Just after Dad died, I sold it all to Joe. He wanted it."

"It worked out, then, for both of you?"

Tom was silent for more than a heartbeat, swiveling his head to check traffic around in with his mirrors. Finally, he answered. "I'm delighted to not have to do law, except in my books. And I'm thrilled to have Joe in town. He likes the small town and almost never leaves. I myself like the trip to New York every few months. Just for a visit. I can't see myself living there."

"I had always thought that's what I wanted, but I never knew there was anything like this, like Abigale, anywhere" She flapped her hands in the air and was quiet for a moment. "My life just got flipped around, and I think I'm going to like it. In the city you don't even know who is living beside you or working beside you. In town, everyone knows everyone, and all their business." She looked intensely at Tom, surprise in her voice. "Gosh. I'm just getting to know my family, but folks in town know all about them."

"It feels secure. I like that about small towns."

"You say that, but how many know about your author career?"

"That. Well, Joe. Josie knows I write, but thinks, like the everyone else, that I'm living off some sort of legacy. See, when two or more know a secret, it has a way of getting out. Joe. He's committed to keeping secrets, what with family law. It's what makes him good at it."

"Do you suppose I'll ever find out the family secrets?"

"If more than one person knew. Someone had to attend the birth of your mother. A midwife, doctor, nurse, someone. That might be a starting point. Births are usually published in the newspapers, but in special circumstances, the mother can choose to not have the birth published. I'd guess this would be the case with this."

"Right. And if she was born in a hospital, there's all those privacy things in place. If she was born at home, well, there'd be no record, anyways."

"Would Anita have been too old to have a child?"

"Maybe. She'd have been about 50-ish."

"Women give birth into their late forties, sometimes."

"True. Who in town is old enough to recall who the midwives were? That might be the best approach, then. And we can hope it was a midwife and not a hospital birth."

"Agreed. I'll ask around. Connect you up."

The Topped Toff

Annie was fatigued when they stopped at the Kennebunkport rest stop. They had a large lunch and then Tom took the wheel for the next three hours of driving.

≡   ≡   ≡

Chapter 21

Annie dropped Tom off and drove the truck to the Dower and slid out. After almost ten hours on the road, she was very glad to arrive. The unloading could wait for the next day.

As she was stretching her legs, she heard loons calling. She wandered down to the beach to catch a glimpse of them. Instead, she saw the family of ducks. There were only five youngsters now, almost indistinguishable from their parents. She took a moment to wonder what had happened to the other five youngsters. When would these be ready to fly away?

Back in the house, she fixed a cup of Oolong tea and went to the journals. 1979, The year her mother was born. The year everything here changed. Was Kelly Marie her grandmother? She scoured the journals of that year to catch any mentions of illness or disruptions. She then went back to the previous year.

There were no references to pregnancy, or illness, or changes, but a few notes of an irate mother. Anita. Anger dominated the comments. Anita was angry with the help, with her absent husband and with her daughters. She railed all the time, by the accounts, about the absent Louise. *"Mother is on a tear again"* or *"mother got her back up today,"* or *"if I hear anymore about Louise not coming home"* were regular posts.

Before August, pages were filled with names of guests, food to be served and clothing to be worn. Kelly Marie had written down funny and smart things her guests had done. The posts about parties and weekend guests stopped at the end of August. It was like someone had shut off a tap and there were no more guests.

Kelly Marie had written about one huge blowout by her mother when her father had arrived, and then nothing. Ever. Nothing more about her father. In November, the entries stopped altogether and didn't pick up again until May of the following year. There were no more mentions of angry outbursts from Anita, no visits from Lucien, no letters from Louise, of Louise coming back to town and no mention of a baby.

In May, just Kelly Marie and Anita were in the house. There was no mention of live-in help. Entries were about groceries delivered, loons and ducks on the lake, repairs to the house after a storm, yard work by a hired hand and books read.

Annie quickly flipped through more journals to see if Lucien or Louise were mentioned. They were not, until 1991. Lucien had died in Boston. There were no details. Kelly Marie made the arrangements. She made a passing note that her mother's memory was becoming spottier, sometimes speaking of Lucien as if he were still alive and living with them. The angry Anita seemed to have disappeared by then. The name Louise didn't appear anywhere.

Anita died in 2005. Kelly Marie still wrote in her journals, but usually about books read or television shows, or ducks and other wildlife. Just after her mother's death, there was a small note about having visited a lawyer and 'taken care of much needed business'. 2006. Annie could only surmise that's when the will naming her as heir to the house was made.

Eyes burning with strain from the driving and the study of journals, Annie put it all away and went to fix a small snack. She then went to bed without turning on her laptop.

She was up and about early the next morning. She wanted the truck emptied and returned. She was on the doorstep trying to figure which door to drive the truck to and how to get that done when she saw Tom's car come down the drive. Two people were in it. She recognized Josie. That would be a help.

Behind Tom's car, she saw another car. It took her a moment, but then she recognized Joanne from the hardware. Tom had apparently enlisted some help.

In no time, the truck was emptied and her hallway and library full of bags and boxes.

As they worked, Annie asked Joanne if she might know who might have been a midwife back in the day.

"Oh, sure. That would have been old Eliza. Women back then were trying to do more natural, at home sort of thing. Midwives were all the rage." She paused with a bag dangling from each hand. "But she'd been trained by her mother who ran the local nursing home in the forties and fifties, back when a nursing home was a place for birthing. Old folks' home was where the elderly went."

Annie paused halfway from the truck to the house with a question. "Right. Anything you know about this?"

Joanne shook her head and started to walk to the house with her bags.

"If I wanted to know something from back then, Eliza is the person? I assume from what you said that she's still with us."

"Yes. Strong and still kicking. She's John's cousin."

"Can you put me in touch with her?"

"Sure. I'll give you the number. You pregnant?" She said it with a chuckle that meant she was joking.

"No," answered Annie vehemently, before she realized Joanne was teasing.

"She'll talk with you. She has information going back generations, as she had helped her mom deliver babies when she was still a child. Women say odd things in labor, you know. I threatened to divorce John the first time, to cut off his, you know, the second time and by the fourth baby, I was threatening to kill him if he ever touched me again. I didn't mean it, or course."

"My mother was apparently adopted." Annie hadn't meant to tell anyone, but it slipped out before she could censor it.

"Oh, I see." Joanne didn't seem surprised.

"Someone must know something. I never knew and now I don't know if she knew."

"Small towns. If you talk to Eliza, bring cookies. She loves cookies. Any kind."

"Thanks."

With all the hands available, the truck was soon ready to return to the rental.

"Thanks, all of you. This might have taken all day. I didn't know they had that slide-y ramp just under the box, and I didn't realize they had the little dolly to use, either."

"Glad to help. Now I go open the store." It was barely nine. "Yes." She shrugged. "We usually don't get any customers until after ten, so we've stopped opening at the cusp of dawn." Joanne turned to go, then turned back to Annie. "Heck, some days we don't get any customers. All going to the city, now. There isn't a business to leave our kids. They've all gone off anyways. See you soon.

Annie waved at them as they left and turned to Tom and Josie. "Thanks to you, too."

"My pleasure, but now I have to go fix lunch for my guests. I left them muffins for breakfast."

She waved as Tom and Josie left, then went back to the shore. She thought she heard loons, but far away. She saw one scooting across the water, sort of flying just over the waves, then it landed back on the lake. She wondered if it was one of the little ones testing its wings.

She used the number Joanne had given and made an appointment for later that day with Eliza. .She cooked some oatmeal raisin cookies for the aging former midwife.

Eliza turned out to be a trim and active senior citizen with a shock of pure white hair. She welcomed Annie with joy at the gift of cookies. They sat on the porch of the century old white on white Victorian in the mild late August air.

"What do you want to know? Most strangers who come here are looking for information they can't get in the public records." She was smiling as she spoke.

"I've just learned that my mother's birth certificate was 'amended'. Do you know anything?"

"You're the new owner of The Dower! You're looking for information on Anita, Kelly Marie and Louise?"

"Right." Annie held her breath. Would it be that easy.

The Topped Toff

"I'll tell you. I was still pretty young, about ten, if I remember. I'd been to lots of deliveries, though. I helped my mother deliver both those girls. Anita was a bitty thing, and I thought it would be a long and difficult delivery. It was just as smooth as it can get. First babies are sometimes slow, but Louise was as easy as pie. And then, a few years later, Kelly Maire was born. Same thing." Eliza focused on eating a cookie. "These are delicious. Not storebought, though I like even those." She took a second cookie but set it on the table in front of them. "Those girls weren't close. Louise left town as soon as she could. But once in a lifetime, magic happens and two people get to be friends." Eliza launched into a recitation of the friendship that developed between her mother and Anita, rattling off some fun times they'd had. "Anita didn't have many close friends near I could tell. She did love to throw parties for her daughters. Well!" She paused and took the cookie she'd put on the table. "These are great. Anyways, as I was saying, Kelly Maire always liked a good time. Her twelfth birthday party, most of the kids in town were invited. It was a real bash. And the parties continued. Swim parties, Fourth of July complete with fireworks, Christmas parties almost every evening in December." Eliza kept adding 'and I remember' when Annie thought she was done.

"I was hired to help with Anita, when Kelly Marie would go away. No one seemed to know where she went. I thought she might have been going to visit her father, maybe Louise, but maybe she had a special friend."

"A friend."

"Sorry. I'm rambling. I was one of the few people who knew that Kelly Marie was pregnant in 1978. That summer, something happened in that house. I was called in about

December, if I remember. Kelly Marie was having a difficult time and had just realized it was because she was pregnant. We never ever spoke of who the father was. I still don't know. I helped with the delivery, filled out the birth certificate and then the child disappeared. I was afraid, at first, that either she or Anita, had done something awful." She paused, a cookie held in her hand like an amulet. "I confronted Anita. She said she didn't know anything about any baby. Then I confronted Kelly Marie. That's when I heard the child had been adopted." She shook her head

"Did you know by whom?"

"I asked more closely, just to be sure. I was told off, told to mind my own business, that the child had a good home, and that was all I needed to know. My midwife days are over, so I'm not harming my reputation by talking about these things, if you know what I mean."

"You seem to remember a lot about it. Anything else you can tell me." Annie started to reach for a cookie, then pulled her hand back and watched Eliza.

I remember it because this one situation was a bit unique for the seventies. Single moms were keeping their kids by then. Back in the forties and fifties, during my mother's era, it was different."

"I've heard it was. I want to thank you for the information. It has been extremely helpful."

"I can't prove, you understand, that your mother was the baby Kelly Marie had, or that Louise adopted the child."

"I know. Still, I have more information now than before."

The Topped Toff

Back home, her head was aswirl. She now was sure her grandmother was not Louise, but Kelly Marie. What was the story behind her pregnancy? That would wait, though it gnawed at her as she started unpacking.

She wondered at the secrets families kept. Her family as well as others. How many children were born and died not knowing their true parents? DNA. She'd do a test to see if maybe she could tag into her grandfather's line.

That left only one really big mystery. The body in the attic. Who and why?

She would have to leave that one to time, as she had no leads.

The name that kept popping up, though, was Claire. Maybe Claire could help her with the missing persons thing. Tom offered to go with her, to ensure there would be no 'lock in'. And just why had Claire locked her in? Annnie was reluctant to go to her, but needed the information Claire might have.

≡ ≡ ≡

Chapter 22

It only took a day to integrate her city possessions into the Dower. Everyone called it that. *The Dower*. It was a term for a house usually titled to a wife when the couple married, as a security if anything should befall the male wage earner. Most often the property was bought with the dowery a woman brought into the marriage, at a time when most women weren't allowed to own property.

So little had she owned in New York. So much did she now own, such a large house. Were there crevices and corners she hadn't explored yet. Might there be a place where something hidden might be found to shed light on what had happened that had changed everything so drastically? She only had word of mouth that Kelly Marie was the sister who was pregnant. Was there proof somewhere? Maybe a missing journal? Had she missed something left behind by Anita?

By days end, she had decided to investigate the house more thoroughly and also to poke through the few papers she had left from her own parents.

The trip and visit with Eliza had left her emotionally exhausted. In just a few short weeks, her life had altered so significantly. Sleep came slowly, at first, but when she heard the loon call, she was able to relax. Her grandmother would have listened to this same sound for all her growing years. Why had she never returned? And why had she adopted Kelly Marie's baby?

Wednesday morning dawned dull and rainy. "A good day to go spelunking in old records," she said to herself.

The Topped Toff

After a light breakfast and coffee, she decided to go searching through the ledgers, which she'd mostly ignored while exploring the journals. She first set them in order chronologically. Then she started at the first ones, which dated from before there was a Dower House. Annie scanned the daily household expenses, bills paid and minor and major purchases.

Anita had done a fine job of bookkeeping and Annie wondered if she'd had some office training. She got a feel for what life was like, when The Dower was bought and furnished and there was a lot of money, big sums, spent. It wasn't always clear what the money had been spent on. Two years in, and the numbers started repeating. It was like the bills got paid twice, and there again were vast amounts spent with no clear reason. About this time, there was a signature at the end of the month, a bookkeeper maybe. Annie could see the dots of ink where the person checked numbers. She could visualize him adding things up. A final total and a signature at the end of every month had become a part of the ledgers. Someone was double checking Anita's expenses. Todd Cash was the name used. The repeat of numbers had her stymied. She'd never seen this as a bookkeeping module.

After a few hours, she called Tom and asked if he'd go with her to see Claire, at the Archives.

He met her at the door. "You sure?" He was grinning as he asked.

"I hope she can answer some questions."

"Do you suppose it could be her husband that ended up in your attic?" His grin turned into a full smile. "After all, he supposedly left her about that time.

"I doubt it."

Claire met them and led them to her office. Once everyone was seated, Claire spoke first. "Can't you just leave the past alone? You women! Anita was as bad as this, too. She couldn't leave well enough alone."

"Like what?"

"If it hadn't been for those wild parties out there to her house, my first husband would never have left me. He'd go out there on a Saturday night and come back with wild ideas."

"About what?"

"What do you think? About what most men think about!" She spat out the word as if it were abhorrent "Money! He had some high-flying scheme to make money from nothing."

Tom spoke softly in an attempt to deescalate the tone. "What did your husband do for work, Claire?"

"He was a tax man. He did taxes for businesses. He was sharp with numbers. But that was all long ago."

"And you are sure he left the area?"

Claire gave him an odd look. Then she nodded. "Oh, you think the body?" She shook her head. "It's not him! He high tailed it out of town, and his secretary was gone the next day. She ran out on her rent. So much for his grandiose ideas about money. Good thing I had a decent job. But I still blame them women out there. But something happened the week before he left. It worried him. Then he was gone."

"But they left?"

The Topped Toff

"Oh, sure. I think he went to Canada, at first. He ended up out West, somewhere. I heard from him after about two years, through Eldred." She nodded at Tom. "Your grandfather. He handed me an envelope one day. There was a letter of apology. Just a few words saying sorry. And there were papers filing for divorce. I signed on the spot. She was in her early twenties, just out of business school. I think they had kids and got married. Maybe not. He never came back to town, that I know of. Now you know all the dirty details. Is there anything else I can help you with." It wasn't a question she was looking for an answer to, but a dismissal.

"Do you recall anything else about those weeks? Anything that changed in town, or out to the house?"

"Those first few weeks things were a bit blurry. When I finally accepted that he was gone, I realized that there was less traffic through town on weekends. I used to look forward to seeing Lucien once or twice a year." She chuckled and stared out the side window for a moment. "It was a pleasure to just look at him. He was a real good-looking man. A real lady killer." She smiled at the recollection. "Funny thing was that he never came to town that I knew of after that one big weekend. He'd just send up that fancy man, to check on the women and pay the bills."

"The bills. A man was hired to pay their bills?"

"Yes. I was employed at the bank, at the time. He'd come in, all city style clothes, and just make out all these cashier's checks. Once a month, like clockwork. By then it had become obvious that Anita had memory problems, nothing big time, just sometimes she'd mix up names, things like that."

"The ledgers. You say you worked at the bank. I worked finance in the city. Can you think of any reason to list expenses twice in a ledger?"

"Twice? Only if you are double dipping."

"Double dipping?"

"Making believe there are expenses that there aren't. I thought you said you'd worked in finance."

"She did." Tom waved towards her, then bit his lip to keep himself quiet.

"I did. It's what I did, what I went to school for."

"We were supposed to watch for it, for anyone paying the same bill twice. Sometimes the method is used for money laundering."

"And did you see anything peculiar from anyone at the Dower?"

"No. They were just real regular. There were a few hiccups after Kelly Marie took over. But she soon had things under control. The spending dropped off, as things quieted down. No more big weekend parties. Course, Louise was gone by this time. I think the celebrations were more by Anita than the girls."

Tom spoke up. "And about when did this happen? That the parties stopped?"

Claire stared at him for a full minute before she decided to answer. "It was late 70's. No, I remember. It was in '79, the year my divorce came through, but what does that matter. That was a long time ago, now."

Tom only nodded, then looked over at Annie. He looked back at Claire. "That would have been when Annie's mother was born. Are you sure it wasn't late in '78?"

"Now that you mention it, it could have been. Well, it was about then, anyways."

Annie thought about it. She looked at Tom. "I'll have to check, but I think that Lucien may have been using the Dower to conceal illicit gains."

Tom's eyes got wide. "Wow."

"Claire, is there any record of the cashier's check from back then?"

"No, honey. Isn't that the point of cashier's checks? We didn't keep anything like that. Once things went digital, it all went down the tubes. Then there was a huge flood in 1987. The town lost a lot of records in the basements. After that, things were moved here from various archives in town, but not from the bank."

"Thank you." Annie nodded at Tom. "I need to go back home and check a few things. I may know what happened. I may even know who was left in the attic. I don't know how he got there, or who shot him, but I think I know who it was."

"Feel free to come peruse the archives at any time. I promise not to lock you in next time." Her smile bordered on evil.

Tom was silent until they were on the road. "Who do you think it is?"

"I'm not sure and I don't want to say until I know. You'll be the first to know, when I am sure."

Back at the house, she again had a go with the ledgers. She first made sure they were in order by date. Then slowly, one at a time she opened them. She compared Januarys across five years, then she went to February, then March. By the time she had reached June, she could see the pattern. Several large checks went out each month to a construction company, listed as paint, dry wall, cement, wall board, replacement of windows, wood treatment. Annie was pretty sure none of that work had ever occurred. Her grandfather Lucien did seem to be running money through the Dower accounts. Did Anita catch on? Kelly Marie?

In August of 1978, the sign offs by the bookkeeper stopped. A few months later, the handwriting changed, so that must have been when Kelly Marie took over the books.

"I almost missed it," Annie said to herself. "You clever jerk." She wondered how much of the fortune left to her were illegal gains. Was there even a way to check something that had happened over fifty years ago?

With a headache threatening, she went out and sat at the shore. Someday, she'd sit and try to figure out how much had been passed though the accounts as if for the house. She'd also check her great grandfather's business in Boston. There must be records somewhere. She was pretty sure Todd Cash was a made-up name.

≡   ≡   ≡

Chapter 23

Annie was visiting with Josie at the inn on Thursday morning. "How could I have not seen it? My expertise is in finance. I will admit I had only glanced at the ledgers. But the whole explanation was there. Anita must have known what Lucien was up to and that would have been what sparked the arguments that Kelly Marie writes about."

"You would have found it sooner or later."

"I think I need to go to Boston and learn about Lucien's business. It does seem he was laundering money using the Dower. I think he may have been a gangster."

"Whatever it was, it's over, now. Apparently, it was over that one weekend in Augusts of 1978."

"That's what I make of it. I think someone killed this Todd Cash. A bullet in the heart is not suicide. Where the body got stashed, how it got half of it dehydrated and half of it defleshed is up for debate. I'll go talk to the corner. He may have insight."

"He's coming to lunch here today. Been slow days for him." Josie's eyes sparkled when she mentioned him.

"Something special?"

"No, the menu is the same." Josie pointed to the menu standing between the salt and pepper shakers.

"I meant you and him?"

"Oh, well, nothing formal. Just, you know." Josie blushed despite her denial.

"He dragging his feet?"

"No, I am."

"Go for it, I say. You never know how long you have."

"That's for sure. But gangster money right here in Abigale?"

"Looks that way."

"Did Claire provide any answers?" Josie looked at her sideways and grinned. "She didn't try to lock you in again?"

Annie shrugged. "Claire blames the women of my family for the loss of her first husband. He used to go out there on weekends, then he'd come home with extraordinary schemes. He left the week after 'it' happened in the Dower, whatever that was. Maybe I'll try to reach out and see if he's still around and ready to talk about it."

"Now, that's an idea. Oh, here comes the lunch troupe. I'm usually closed on Thursday, but the book club made reservations. I'll talk with you later." Josie went to the first table and took the order.

Annie left and went to see Joe at the law office, the office that had handled Claire's divorce. Maybe they'd have an address for Claire's ex.

The all-white house that served as office was locked with a note that office hours were Monday, Wednesday and Friday noon to five, except by appointment. Annie rang the doorbell anyway. No one answered and she left. Joe wasn't in.

Annie didn't want to go back to Claire with questions about the ex-husband, so she thought maybe she'd try Julie at the newspaper. After all, a newspaper was a great place to gather gossip.

The Topped Toff 185

Again, she was disappointed. A sign on the door with a placard said Julie would be back at two. Annie left a note on the door for Julie to call her.

Back at the house, she found herself by the lake, for a few minutes, but then went in to tackle more of the ledgers. It was now plain to her that the entries seemed to feed money back into the companies that were allegedly fronts. Might those companies be owned by Lucien.

In the month of August 1978, she saw something she hadn't seen before. Minute red dots, which she'd thought to be red marking pen, but now thought they were blood spots. Had the man been murdered while cooking the books. Who had caught him? Had Anita known what the Dower really was? Was that why Louise had left and not returned? Had Kelly Marie found out? So many unanswered questions.

Joe was the first to call. "I can't give you details, but I've been handling Claire's estate, and her ex- has died. She'd know that, as she's been collecting on his social security the past five years." He asked how the trip had gone and then his tone changed. "My three o-clock is here. Talk to you later."

Julie called next. They chatted for a few minutes. "I'm too young to recall anything like that. What did the corner say? Can they identify him yet."

Annie told her about the apparent double entries and all the construction payments with no apparent work being done and the mystery man who signed as Todd Cash.

"Look for any person in your grandfather's life with the T C initials. In all the mystery novels, people often stay somewhere near the truth when making up a name."

"Thanks. I'm going to hunt around and see if Lucien left anything. Any of his 'stuff' would have landed here. There might be a box of papers somewhere that I've overlooked."

"Sure, sure. Look, someone just came in."

Again, Annie was disappointed. She really didn't know where to turn. She'd learned all she could from Eliza the midwife and from Claire, the records keeper, and Joe the lawyer, which wasn't much.

She was running her hand over the cover of a ledger when it occurred to her to take it to the coroner to confirm that it was blood on the page, and maybe get a definitive answer that the blood came from the corpse found at the top of her house.

"Oh, my," said Mark "Let me test it. Theres' enough I can test and still have some for a DNA. We'll see in a minute." Mark was fortyish, tall and rail thin.

Annie sat to wait, but popped up and nervously paced the small office.

In just a moment, he returned. "Yup. Blood. I'll run a DNA test, and I think I'll run this by Dave, too. I mean, there was obviously a crime, so this might relate. Well, most likely it will. I mean, who bleeds over an account book?" He was reaching for swabs in a tube as he spoke. "It won't be long before we know for sure. I was able to get some good DNA from the bones of the victim. I'll call you when we know." It was a dismissal.

The Topped Toff

Annie was at loose ends about what to do next. She went out to the house and sat by the water. Had her grandmother sat here? She had thought of Lousie as grandmother, and in effect she was, but most likely Kelly Marie was her birth grandmother. In either case, Anita and Lucien were grandparents. Then, she thought about who might have been her mother's father. Was it the mysterious Todd?

She jumped up and went in. "Mark. Can you take my DNA and match to a grandfather?"

"Yes. Grandfathers are easy. But I don't have your grands."

"You might."

Oh, you think---?"

"What if---what if that's what if he was lovers with Kelly Marie?"

"You think maybe he took advantage?"

"Oh, my. What if? Kelly would have been in her mid-twenties. Todd was her father's man. He had been coming to the house one weekend a month for years. What if that's why Louise left? He was taking advantage of the girls?"

"I deal in facts, not supposes, but it is possible."

"I'm going to do a thorough search of this house, looking for any telltale clues."

"I would look for blood pools under rugs, between floorboards. Look, why don't I come out. We'll do our own CSI hunt."

Annie chuckled. "Sure. Bring your sprayee stuff, black light and all. Bring your appetite. I'll make us supper."

"It's a plan. See you after I get off work, about sixish, maybe?"

"Done." Her next move was to also invite Josie out for the hunt. "All hands on deck, as they say," she told Josie.

After her phone calls and starting a beef stew in her crockpot, she went up into the attic. Time to scour and see if she'd missed anything. The gap in journals from Kelly Marie was like a missing tooth that you keep shoving your tongue into. She had trouble thinking that the detailed record keeping would have ceased during such a momentous thing as pregnancy and delivery of the child, adoption stuff, and then resumed as if nothing had happened with no mention of it.

Up in the attic again, she slowly went through things. The trunks, dressers and wardrobes, not so much looking at the old clothes and trinkets left from previous generations, this time, but searching for hidden spaces that might hold journals, notes, letters and ledgers. Methodically, she started at one end of the large attic and slowly worked her way along one side, then down the other. She saw nothing she hadn't seen before. She found no love letters, no bills or receipts, no delivery invoices, nothing with any information and no secret compartments.

Feeling a bit defeated, she yet looked forward to a visit from Mark, the coroner, and his *'close friend'*, Josie. She chuckled at her subterfuge to get them together outside the inn. It might be interesting, if not productive.

The stew was ready, and she put the crockpot on 'warm' and changed out of her dusty clothes and combed her short hair.

The Topped Toff

She set her small kitchen table for three and set up the counter buffet style. They'd search for blood spatter would start after supper. An image of a 'haunted house' movie made her chuckle. But what could go bump in the night in this house? She wasn't afraid of ghosts, but what might the hunt reveal. Might she learn of her 'real' grandfather?

Josie was the first to arrive. "What a beautiful day."

"You arrived early. Welcome."

"We didn't have any guests, and I'm closed for supper on Thursday. It's my day to prepare for the new clients who come on Friday, usually. And they stay to Wednesday or early Thursday."

Mark arrived shortly after. "Well, hey there, you two. Thick as thieves, are we? And are we going to witch hunt or is it ghost hunting?"

Josie's eyes flashed at his cleverness. "Looking for clues. Maybe a genealogical spelunking?"

Annie could have been anywhere else. The two kept up the repartee and teasing through the meal.

"Now, where to?" Josie stood and was clearing dishes from the table.

"Oh, leave it. I'll clean up after, or tomorrow or whenever."

"Sorry! Habit!"

Mark stood. "Lead the way. I always wanted to see what this house looked like inside. I used to sometimes come out here to eat lunch and listen to the wildlife. You'd be surprised how much there is even in winter when the lake is frozen. It's gorgeous."

"Hey, just cause I'm here, you can still come out. I'm going to set out some of those chairs that lean a little back."

"Adirondack."

Annie didn't catch it. "Bless you."

"No, Adirondack is the name of the chair."

"Got it." She nodded at him once. "I thought we'd start in the library. I've already checked every drawer in the desk."

Mark looked around the library in wonder. "A lot of books. Are these all yours?"

"No. Well, they are now, but they were mostly here. I just unpacked them from where they'd been stored. Ready, set, go."

Mark flirted with both women, but mostly Josie, as they all flipped through books. It took an hour.

Annie left for a few minutes and came back with three beers.

"Ah, refreshments." Mark and Josie were standing close, but not very close. "I'll take one of those."

"Me too," said Josie as she eagerly reached.

The searching ceased. "We've gone through all of them. No hidden journals, love letters, death threats or confessions."

"Gotcha."

The three sat and sipped beer in silence.

Josie jumped up and started opening the desk drawers.

Annie shook her head. "I've checked the desk several times. Nothing but empty."

The Topped Toff

"These old desks sometimes had secret compartments."

"I've been aware of those on the old roll tops, but this isn't that old, just a flat top."

"Mark, got your tape?"

"Have tape will travel." He reached into his back pocket and pulled out a small retractable seamstress style tape measure and handed it to Josie.

Annie wondered about the intimacy of such knowledge.

Josie measured each drawer, then she measured the inside, too. "Here. There's a four-inch difference between the outside and the inside." She pulled on the drawer to remove it, but it only went so far.

"Let me," said Mark.

≡　　≡　　≡

Chapter 24

Mark knelt by the lower drawer and leaned over to see inside of it. He then put his hand out and pulled it back quickly. "Ouch! That hurt." He looked at his hand and put a finger in his mouth to absorb the spot of blood.

"What. What happened? You hurt?" Annie stepped closer.

"No, just a pin prick. Hopefully it isn't laced with poison."

"Be careful," said Josie.

Mark put his hand back in the drawer, more cautiously. "A flashlight, please?"

"Oh, sure. Let me go get one."

"Phone?" Josie handed him her phone which she'd switched to flashlight mode.

"Thanks." He leaned in and examined the drawer. "I see the latch." He carefully reached in and triggered the release and the drawer slid out. He placed the drawer on the desk. In that position, it was obvious that the floor of the drawer was higher than the bottom.

"Oh, my."

All three people stepped up to the desk and examined the drawer as if it were some exotic animal on display.

"There." Josie pointed. "That's the latch to open the bottom."

Annie turned the drawer on its side, then she sprung the small latch. A cascade of journals and papers and letters spread across the desk and tumbled onto the floor. "Oh, my."

The Topped Toff 193

"Told you." Josie was standing back as if the drawer had teeth.

Mark bent and started picking up those items that had drifted to the floor.

Annie picked up a journal and scanned it. "Kelly Marie's, for sure. It's her handwriting." She went to the date of her mother's birth in the third journal she picked up. April 10, 1979. "Look. The birth is here." She read silently for a minute. "Oh." Another minute passed. "Oh."

"What is it?" asked Josie.

"It is the record of mother's birth. *'Baby born this morning at three o'clock. An easy birth, I'm told.'* What does that mean?"

"Kellie Marie wasn't the mother?" Josie leaned over to read over Annie shoulder. "Maybe she wasn't even there."

"Maybe," said Mark. He picked over the papers that had been found in the drawer. "Mostly letters. Here's one dated about six months before the birth. Appears to be from Louise to Kelly Marie."

Annie took it from him. "That's Gram's handwriting."

Annie opened it and read aloud. "*'I'll be up before the birth. We'll sort things out. Ed is agreeable. Thrilled, actually. Don't you worry. It will all turn out well.'* Nothing else."

"That isn't helpful." Josie was handling the various journals, glancing at the dates and putting them back. "Look, these are all from that time that the pregnancy occurred, whomever was carrying the child. Maybe it was Anita. She might have been young enough."

Annie looked over. "She would have been about fifty. Maybe."

"Here it is." Annie held up a piece of paper. "This is the birth certificate, from before it was altered. "Oh, Kelly Marie. Father is *unknown*."

"That used to be how it was done when the mother didn't want to tell who the father is." Mark was handling more of the paperwork. "Maybe she'll name him in the journals."

Josie had opened the first of the four journals that had been in the drawer. She read the first entry out loud *"I've been begging mother to stop having these wild parties. She's been giving parties since we were very young. She'd invite the whole class, if not the whole school including parents and teachers. Later, she'd invite our college acquaintances for the weekend. I begged her to stop. I think that's why Louise left. She'd invite all these people and then she'd go missing for an hour, or for the evening, along with one of the guests. I'd find guests paired off in one or another of the rooms, as if she'd given everyone permission to be free about the house."*

Now Annie was leaning over and reading over Josie's shoulder.

Josie read silently for a moment, turned the page, and then started up again, her finger halfway down the page. *"I wasn't feeling well and went to my room, or did someone take me there? Anyways, he was on me, my clothes were off, and it hurt and I tried to ask him to stop, but couldn't talk and then it ended, but I could see people in the doorway. Or did I imagine that."*

"Oh, gosh," said Mark.

Josie quickly thumbed to the next page. "She talks about how she dislikes sex, and why are folks so all hyped up about it, and it hurts."

"What a horrible thing." Annie was holding her fist to her mouth and tears were threatening. "A wild party sponsored by her mother, who would go off alone with a guest. Possible rape by one of those attending. Pregnancy which was followed by adoption." Annie sat with a thud. "I feel as if the world I've been in has morphed and I'm in another universe as someone else."

Josie put a hand on her shoulder. "Are you all right?"

Annie picked up the journal Josie had been reading from. She reread the entry. "No wonder this was hidden." She flipped the page. "Oh, gosh. This may be it. Look."

Josie and Mark peered over each shoulder, with a hand on opposite shoulders, twining the three together.

Annie read some more. "*I heard a loud bang. I don't remember anything else. It must have been Mother closing my door. In any case, everyone was gone the next morning when I woke up. It was as if I'd dreamt it all, including father being here.*"

Mark was going through the documents still on the desk. He held one up. "*Another letter from Louise. 'You need to contact father. He can put an end to Mother's doings.' Further on, 'This is a legal matter. He'll pull strings to make it happen.'*"

Annie shifted her gaze to Mark. "It seems Louise knew Lucien had some sort of influence. Too bad he didn't use it before things got out of hand."

"Whatever Lucien did, we know things did change about that time. Everyone in town knows the parties stopped. Now we know the reason."

"You can't tell anyone." Annie was in a panic about gossip spreading.

"I wouldn't. Nor would Mark. Right Mark?" Josie looked up at him intensely.

"Mum's the word with me. No reason for anyone to know."

Josie took the journal from Annie. "A loud bang. Might that have been the shot that killed our victim?"

Mark now shifted and was looking over Josie's shoulder. "Let me see. Could have been, I suppose. If so, I wonder who shot him, and where the gun went."

Josie read aloud from a few pages further on. "*I know I'm pregnant. It happened that night when things got fuzzy. I'm not sure what happened. Well, I can guess. I think I was drugged. I didn't know half of the people there. I'm not even sure mother did.*"

Annie palmed tears off her cheeks. "This house holds secrets well."

"Secrets plural, for sure." Josie sat beside Annie and put a hand on hers on the chair arm. "What now? What are you going to do with this?"

"I'm going to submit my DNA. Maybe we can worm a way into the family from my grandfather. That might identify who he was. Kelly Marie didn't seem to know."

"Maybe we can find out who was here on that weekend and maybe they'll remember something?" Mark watched Annie to see if she would react to his suggestion.

"That's a great idea," said Annie."

Marc was scanning the third journal from the drawer. "Here's some more information. '*Mother seems more vague and lost these days. The parties have stopped but it is as if her focus on this world has vanished. She wanders the house touching things, moving them a quarter inch and moving on.*' The entry ends there. The next one is more mundane. '*I've taken over meal prep, as our maid seems to have left. If she told Mother she was leaving, I was never told.'* Then there are a few blank pages with just the date, as if she meant to write and didn't."

"She must have felt as displaced as I'm feeling at that point."

Marc picked up a piece of paper from the floor. "So how would you go about finding out who was here?"

Annie responded. "Townsfolks. Someone would remember seeing someone in town. I'll go ask Julie if she knows someone who might have been around and is still with us."

"My aunt, who ran the inn before me, she would have probably known who was in town but not staying here. She's been gone for over five years now. Gosh, I miss her."

"I'll get with Julie first thing."

Josie shook her head. "The minute you start talking with anyone, they'll know. I think Claire may already be conjecturing with her genealogy group."

Marc nodded. "I'd say the half-decomposed body with a bullet in the heart is hard to cover up."

Annie attempted to smile. "I get it. I'll just have to dive in, I guess. Wish me luck."

Josie and Mark said it at the same time. "Good luck." They looked at each other and chuckled and soon all three were laughing.

Annie stood and gathered things and put them in the drawer, but not in the secret compartment. "I've found nothing of Lucien's. That should have all come here, at some point, after he died?"

Louy Castonguay

"All, as in what?"

"All, as in clothes, papers, ledgers. He seemed to be a record keeper. There are ledgers from the Dower, none from his business. Did I miss something?"

"We've scoured the attic. We've scoured the books and this desk holds no more secrets."

"They would have discarded the clothes?" Josie was sitting casually in an end chair.

Mark was still standing, watching the two women.

"Yes. The clothes. Personal effects? A watch, his wallet, ID's, things like that." Annie was gazing at a wall. Tom helped put up the painting where he remembered they all were before the house was closed up. She was silent, still staring at the blank wall.

Marc didn't understand her comment. "And, so what?"

Josie filled in the blanks for him. "In films, there's always a wall safe hidden behind paintings. Do we know there aren't any of those. What about a secret room? Or closet we haven't found?"

"No doors I know of that we haven't opened."

"In the cellar?" Josie was now staring at the place that Annie was, on the wall. "Do you think someone made a hidden room in the cellar?"

"I haven't fully explored that. It's dark and dank and huge."

Mark picked up one of the journals from the box and riffled through it. "Look, here's a few pages ripped out. I hadn't paid attention to it at first, but there are a few dates missing. She wrote and then she tore it out."

The Topped Toff

"I wonder what it was. Well, we won't solve this evening. I'm grateful that you came over."

"Our pleasure, for sure." Mark nodded to Josie.

Josie turned towards the door. "If we can be of any more help. And Tom might be able to help with the basement. Not me, that's for absolute sure."

"I'll do basements only if I have to. Let me know." He was already headed to the door.

Josie followed.

After seeing her guests out, Annie went back into the library and started poking and probing the desk, searching for other hidden compartments, left alone with the family detritus that had been revealed in the hidden compartment in the drawer.

She found nothing. Admitting defeat, she turned to leave. "Julie, first. Basement eventually," she said to the empty room.

≡ ≡ ≡

Chapter 25

Annie slept poorly that night. Her sleep was interrupted with dreams of things hidden in the huge house. She had first seen when it was empty out and wondered where in the house someone might hide things. She'd searched all possible places.

The call of loons just after dawn was like a homecoming serenade. She finally drifted off to a restful sleep, only to be awakened by a voice calling to her from below her bedroom window. After she finally chased the fuzzies from her brain, she realized it was Tom.

"Hey there, sleepy head. Let me in. Wakey, wakey."

She stumbled up and went to the window and opened it. "Hey, be down in a minute."

He nodded and headed around to the door.

She jammed herself into some clothes and raced down to open the front door. "What is so important to wake me?"

"Ah, I could have just come in, but didn't want to give you a fright."

"I had that last night, when we found some hidden journals."

"I heard about that at breakfast."

"What time is it?" She was reaching for the coffee maker to prep it.

"Almost noon. Hard night?" He took the carafe from her and filled it, allowing her to put the grounds in the basket. With the coffee started they both sat at the table.

The Topped Toff

"Yes. Sleep wasn't easy. I'm wondering where in this house someone might have hidden something. And I guess I might have to go to Boston to see what Lucien really did for work."

"No need to go. I did forensic work while in college. I spent a bit of time in Boston doing research. I'll help. We can access newspaper archives online, and also tax records, property deeds, stuff like that."

She rubbed her forehead. "I just never had to deal with anything like this. Numbers. That's my jam."

"I've not seen anything from Lucien. When he died, wouldn't his stuff have been sent here? To family, I mean? Unless he had other family?"

"That is what I'd expect. And no, I never saw any of his things. Of course, I didn't come to work here until after he'd died. They could have disposed of his personal stuff, maybe."

"Who might know. Is there anyone?"

After a moment of thought, he nodded. "Old Harold Jones. He was the town handyman, carpenter, and general 'get it done', and I think he did some work out here. He might know of something. Maybe some old building since torn down, or a hidey hole in the basement."

"And where is Harold? Is he still around."

"Oh, sure. He's living in the old age apartments up on High Street."

"Will he remember. I mean old folks and all."

"Last time I saw him, a month or so ago, he was walking a dog for a neighbor. He likes to make himself useful, even now. He seemed to know where he was and even knew who I was."

"That's good, isn't it?"

"I'll take you over after lunch. You are going to feed me lunch, aren't you? Or shall we go to Josie's?"

"Are you asking me to lunch?"

"I guess I am." He stood and poured coffee, then turned to her. "Oh, I hope you don't mind."

"No. I just feel so behind everything. I'm having trouble getting up to speed, not something I'm used to. When I first entered this house, there was nothing. No pictures to hide a safe, no rugs to cover up a floor safe, no loose boards that I noticed, and I've gone through all the books in the library, last night. We found a false bottom on a drawer in the desk. It held a few journals, from the time of the pregnancy. We know for sure that Kelly Marie had a child and was most likely my birth grandmother. She doesn't name the person and may not have known him. From what she recorded, she was drugged. But there are pages missing. Mark tells me I'm not a DNA match to the dead person."

"All that means is what that means."

"And what is that supposed to mean?" Puzzled, she looked at Tom. The absurdity of the comment struck her funny bone and she giggled. "This puzzle has me baffled."

Tom smiled. "Nice one." They'd finished their cup of coffee. "Let's go see if Josie will fix us some sandwiches and then go see Harold. He may know of some built-in something we can't see."

The Topped Toff

"Let's."

Josie always served limited menus. She didn't have a restaurant proper. She usually offered several items for each meal. After the meet and greet, she brought them both corned beef sandwiches with coleslaw on it and a side of oven fries. It was the end of the lunch rush and she sat with them.

"Oh, sure, I remember Harold. I still see him from time to time. I didn't know he used to work for the Weeks. But it doesn't surprise me. He had his hand in lots of things, back in the day. He still does a few odd jobs, like walking dogs and watering plants for people who are away. Everyone trusts Harold. He's not a talker, if you know what I mean."

After lunch, the two went off, leaving Josie to clean up after the lunch crowd.

Harold was home and glad to see them. "Hi, Tom. How's things? Read your latest. Good work, that. Making a living yet? I recall the row you had with your old man when he found out you were writing rather than tending the lawyer business."

Annie's eyebrows shot up and she looked at Tom.

He shook his head no. "Later," he told her. "Harold, this is Annie, and she's got the old Dower."

"Oh, my. I didn't think anyone was left to own that old pile. After Kelly Marie died, it was left, wasn't it? Always afraid some developer would come and tear it down. Is that what you are?"

"Actually, I'm Kelly Marie's child, apparently, from what we can figure."

"Kelly Marie? Now there was an odd duck. So shy. And after old Anita went off the rails, we almost never heard from her. Of course, I'd go out and tend whatever she needed. Wasn't much. Mow the grass, plow the yard. That was back before my back trouble. If I recall, she had groceries delivered once a week. They had an older lady out to help with Anita for a while. Then they had some out-of-town agency helping Kelly Marie when she got older. There was a sister who went missing." He saw the look of alarm on Annie face. "I don't mean like as in missing. She moved away and no one around seems to know where or anything." He stared up at the pictures on his wall. "After my missus died, I tried to keep busy. Odd jobs. Some carpentry. Stuff like that."

"We were wondering," Tom pointed to Annie.

"The missing Louise was apparently my adoptive mom."

Tom took up the questions. "We found nothing of Lucien's. Any idea what business he was in?"

"Oh, that's easy. He worked for some outfit in Boston. Let me think. It was a long time ago, and I didn't meet him but once or twice. Insurance? Something financial? Or maybe properties? I'll have to think about it."

"That's beside the point. We have questions about his things. We found nothing of his in the house." Tom again waved at Annie to include her. "We can figure out what he did later. What we really want to know is if any of his stuff came up here after he died, and what the women would have done with it."

"Trunks in the attic. They had me haul one up. It smelled funny, like a ton of mothballs. Maybe that would be it?"

The Topped Toff

"Ah, I think that might have been the body. Do you remember when that might have been?"

"Sure. It was the year my Martha got sick, the first time. 1978. Late in the year. It was cold in the attic. It was always cold in the attic, except when it was broiling hot in summer." Harold rambled on about the sickness of his wife, and the two let him wander memory lane. They now knew when the truck went into the attic.

After a while, Tom brought him back to the issue at hand. "So, you brought the trunk with the body up to the attic?"

"A body, you say? Surely not old Lucien. I saw him a few times after that. He hired me, on retainer, to look after things. I mean, I'd done work out there before. The old lady was a little confused sometimes, and the daughter not much better."

"So, 1978. Just before my mother was born." Annie wished Harold would get more to the point.

Tom made a slowdown motion where only she could see it. "Can you tell us if you ever made any renovations to the house?"

"Sure. That man of Lucien's. The one who was around, but usually only on weekends. What was his name? Something money. No, that's not right. A long time ago, my friend. No, Cash was his last name. I didn't have much to do with him. But he had me out a few times. Demanding, he was. Expected me to drop everything and just go out there. Of course, after Lucien put me on retainer, I did. There was one time. They had me build this space under the floor in the office. I suspect a floor safe went in there. I never saw it, just had to build the space, three feet down, three feet across. Extra strong, using two by sixes, is what I was told. I did. Is it still there?"

Tom nodded, pretending he knew about it to encourage Harold to keep talking.

"They wanted it four feet away from the wall. I told them it would be easier and sturdier to build it into the wall, or even just near the wall. Nope, not what they wanted."

Tom nodded.

"There was a wall safe, too. I installed the hole for that, and later, I came back and put wallboard covering it up. Apparently, no one was supposed to have access to that one. Now why would someone install a safe and then cover it? In the kitchen pantry, it was. At first, I thought it was a hole for the new-fangled microwave oven, but they had me shore it up, too. It was smaller. Only two by two." He stared out through the window. "Of course, the real safe was in the old lady's closet. Or maybe that one was the decoy. I didn't do much in the house after Lucien died. 1990? Maybe '92. I'm not sure. In any case, most everything after that was just outdoor work. And that smart young Cash person stopped coming around, too."

Tom and Annie allowed Harold to wander memory lane a little longer before excusing themselves.

"Holy Cow." Tom was bringing Annie back to the Dower. "This I gotta see. But there was no safe in Anita's closet that I ever saw."

"I don't even know what room she was in. But there was no safe in any closet. I can't wait to check, though. I see a hole where one might have been in the pantry. I thought, like Harold, it was for a microwave. Just no safe there anymore."

When they reached the house, Tom dug around in the back of his vehicle and came out with a carpenter's tape measure. "Let's go find us some safes."

☰   ☰   ☰

Chapter 26

Annie examined the space in the pantry while Tom went to the office and tapped the floor, trying to find the space where the safe was or had been, under the floor.

Annie returned to the library. "I was right. There's a space but no safe in the pantry. Baking pans are now in the cut-out area Harry told us about. I can see where it had been walled up and the wallboard pulled down. I thought you said you were the one who did the work around here for Kelly Marie."

"I did. I worked with dad for her last few years Harry said it was there, so it was pulled out before Dad took over, but after Harry stopped working here. Maybe it was pulled by that Cash person. Or Lucien did it on one of his trips up."

"Tom, the timelines don't seem to work. If Cash is our dead body, when did your dad take over from Harry?"

"You're right. Dad would have taken over in like the '90's. The late 90's. I started coming with him when I was like ten. Lucien was already gone by then. Anita was, she was very feeble and gone soon after."

"And Kelly Marie died in what, like 2012? She would have known, then?"

"Very most likely. Who knows. Maybe my father took them out. Before I started coming here. He never said, though."

Tom was tapping the floor even as they spoke.

"Any luck here?" Annie could see he hadn't found anything yet.

The Topped Toff

"I haven't found any hallows. I'm still working my way around. It would have been helpful to know where in the room the safe was concealed. Harry didn't seem to remember the exact location."

"Doesn't that seem a little, I don't know, a little sketchy?"

"I thought so, but he gave us what he felt comfortable with. Maybe this safe was also taken up."

"Three safes. We can't find even one of those."

"Let's check the dimensions of the house."

"Why?"

"There might be a hidden room."

"What do you mean, a hidden room?"

"It was the old fashion way of hiding things. Called a priest hole, or safe rooms, these days, or slave holes along the underground railroad. These old houses had all sorts of secret places."

"Oh, fine. How can I help?"

"Hold the end of the tape. We'll measure each room, then the outside of the room."

The measured and measured. They started with the library. Room by room, they measured the house, putting the numbers on paper, drawing out the dimensions of the house.

When they finished downstairs, they went upstairs. The rooms appeared the right size. Tom measured the upstairs hallway and added up the inside measurements of rooms on both sides, as well as the closets. "Got it. I just don't know which room. Look. The total size of the hallway and what the inside of the rooms should add up to. There's a discrepancy of like three feet on the left."

"Which room? They seem to be the same inside and outside."

"Oh, clever. It's in the closets, which are nestled side by side."

"That *is* clever."

"I'll go get my tools. Be back in an hour." He sprinted down the stairs and out the door.

Annie heard his car peel out of the drive. She went to the closet and started tapping the walls like she'd seen Tom doing on the floor in the library. She stopped after a few minutes because she didn't know what she was listening for. She went to the kitchen, took out the crockpot and started a chicken stew. Right after she finished prepping and turned on the crockpot, her phone rang.

"I just saw Tom go tearing past going one way and then right back. Know anything about that?" Josie sounded amused.

"We think we found a secret room. Old Harold, who used to work here, told us about safes that were installed, but we didn't find them, so went looking for secret rooms, and I think we found one upstairs between two rooms, hidden in the ends of closets."

"Exciting."

"I've started a chicken stew, if you want to come out to supper. We should know what's in there by then."

"Oh, yes. I'm available. I don't have any clients here at the time."

The Topped Toff

Annie heard Tom enter. "Gotta' go. Talk later?" She hung up and followed Tom upstairs.

He was carrying tools in a large wooden toolbox. He set it down and took out a power saw with a short chain driven bar on it, looking like a toy chain saw. "This should get us in." He went to work in the end wall in the closet.

Annie watched closely, expecting the saw to hit metal.

Going only inches deep, Tom cut a two-foot square. Taking a metal bar out of the toolbox, he peeled off the wallboard. "There you go. A space which is deeper than just the four inches the wall should be.

"Wow. See anything?"

Tom grabbed a mag light from the toolbox. He peered into the space. Up, side to side, then down. "Yup. I think our missing safes are here. Gosh. We would probably never have found them, if we hadn't suspected they existed."

Tom widened the opening. He worked around the wall framing and cut the wall board. "These old houses were built using lathes and horsehair mixed into a compound of plaster of Paris. After a certain number of years, it all turns crumbly. This is not that. This is drywall sheets." He continued cutting. Near the bottom, he hit wood behind the wall board, cut around it and inside of the framing that made a four by four 'hole'. He removed wall board as he went.

Annie fetched a garbage bag and put the detritus in it.

"There. There's your safe."

"Look. Two of them."

"Do you have the combination or the keys? These older safes could be opened with the key."

"I don't recall any keys of any kind. Just the ones you gave me, which go to the doors."

"Check again. Weren't there a few smaller keys?"

Annie ran to her room and pulled the keys from the side table, then hurried back to Tom. "You were right."

Tom huffed and puffed as he finally pulled the larger safe out. "Maybe you're rich. There may be a fortune in here." It was a tease, as he knew she had enough money coming to her to make life very easy.

"As if." She handed him the set of keys. "I thought these were just to old post office boxes or jewelry boxes, or even locking luggage."

Tom found the right key for the safe.

"Papers. Just papers. You'd think it was something extremely valuable to be in a safe hidden in a wall." Annie reached for the papers.

"You sure you want to know. Once you know something, there's no going back. Maybe Lucien was a murderer, and you have that in your bloodline? A hit man for the Mafia?"

"Oh, you." She hit him on the arm.

Just then the doorbell rang. They heard the front door open and a "Yohoo! Anybody home?"

"Up here." Annie responded to Josie's call. "Just in time. Come on up."

Annie again reached for the papers. She scanned the ones on top. "Look. It's the missing pages from Kelly Marie's

The Topped Toff

journals. Oh, my. I think I know why these are here, hidden." Annie spoke first. "Kelly Marie wrote that she thought her mother had shot someone. Here in the house."

Tom had taken a clutch of other papers and was examining them. "These seem to be something else. Oh, shoot." He went quiet but continued to read quietly.

Josie stood behind Tom and read over his shoulder. "Oh, my. Oh, my gosh."

"Right. Oh, goodness," said Tom.

Annie didn't look up at the other two. "I don't know why this wasn't destroyed."

Josie shifted and started looking over Annie's shoulder. "Oh, my."

Annie held out a sheet of paper. "I have something here that looks like something by Anita."

Josie went back to looking over Tom's shoulder. Then she reached for more papers on the small pile. As she unfolded a letter that had been in an envelope, she looked at Annie, then Tom. "What does all this mean?"

"It means" said Annie, "that we know someone was killed here in this house by Anita. We know that because this is her confession."

"But this is a confession that Kelly Marie killed someone. The man who raped her." Josie held out the letter.

"Now I'm confused. We know that man in the attic isn't my grandfather. DNA told us that. If the man who apparently raped Kelly Marie isn't the father of her child, then who is. And who really killed him? And why? We have two confessions. Which one is real." Or is there another body?

Tom put down his papers and reached for another. "*'I killed Z Greener as he was a pain in the side of Lucien, trying to blackmail him by threatening to do the women harm. I found him at the house, bothering the ladies. I then stowed his body in the freezer until Lucien can take care of it. He claims he can make it disappear.'* It's signed Todd Cash."

"Oh, my." Annie went to take the paper from him, then pulled her hand back.

"We have a problem. Three people confessed to the same murder. Why would they do that." Josie leaned her hip on the nightstand.

Tom held out the items he had. "It was evidence in case it was needed. Then, it was hidden, thinking it might never be necessary."

Annie put her paper down, then picked it back up. "Needed for what?"

"Reasonable doubt." Tom held his papers at arms length. "Most of this is bogus. It would plant reasonable doubt at a trial of any of them. But there was no trial, because Lucien did make the body vanish, somehow. And these must have then been hidden when it was obvious that there would be no trial."

"He was killed because he threatened Lucian."

"And the women." Tom just stood quietly. "So much drama. Everyone thought the girls were just having a great time."

The Topped Toff

Josie put her papers back on the pile. "What did this man have on Lucien to use for blackmail?"

"Are you sure you want to go digging into that?"

"I hope my DNA test will uncover the father of my mother. Meanwhile, I'm going to dig to find what Lucien did for work."

"There's another safe in here. Want to examine that, too." Tom walked over to the opening.

"Another hidden safe. Gosh. Most people don't even have one." Josie went behind him and peered into the space.

Annie nodded, though the two others couldn't see her from the closet. "Another. Let's. Can't be as bad as this one."

≡   ≡   ≡

Chapter 27

Tom pulled the second and smaller safe from the hole in the wall in the closet. The trio sorted keys and finally found the appropriate key and opened the second safe.

"Mostly ledgers. They seem to be coded." Tom handed one to Annie.

Josie grabbed one, and Tom chose a third one. They flipped through them.

"I'm a finance person and I can't figure them out. The numbers don't make any sense. I'll need to study these. They are not in the handwriting of those downstairs. I think the downstairs ones were done by the Anita, and then by Kelly Marie. Nor are they in Lucien's handwriting if we compare to these documents, so maybe a bookkeeper, someone working with Lucien?"

There were ten ledgers. A white business envelope at the bottom was addressed 'To Whom It Might Concern'."

Tom pulled it out, looked at it and handed it to Annie. "Want to do the honors?"

Annie opened it. It held one sheet of paper. "Lucien's handwriting. A bit of typing at the top, then a note by him." She continued to read, then read it aloud.

"'By the power of myself, vested in me by myself, I deed this safe and all it contains to whomever is clever enough to find it. I hope all parties to this madness is gone by then. Do with it as you will.'. I am a businessman primarily, but after Anita and I agreed to live apart, I took on a few ambiguous businesses to my accounting practice. I wanted to leave a great legacy for my two daughters, Louise and Kelly Marie. Both, as far as I know, are my natural daughters. So, I then

did things I maybe should not have and before I knew, my wife's Dower House, a place I'd gotten for her to have as her very own, was being used to recycle some money from enterprises that I wasn't knowledgeable about. I can only guess. Forward a few years, and the business I was dealing with started to threaten my family if I didn't continue to cooperate. I distanced myself from family, hoping to keep them safe, but the threats continued. I then took care of things.

This is a full confession. I killed Zerry Greens and threw his body in an old root cellar on the property. I later had my man, my best friend, Todd Cash, move the remains to another location, bidding him not tell me where. On the night that I killed Zerry, he had thrown a party at The Dower, for his men, to show me he was boss, and a man raped my daughter, Kelly Marie. That man is also now a missing person, who will never be found in my lifetime, if ever. My only regret is that I didn't do away with Zerry before he turned his thugs loose in my wife's house." Annie turned the sheet of paper over. "That's all."

Josie peered over her shoulder. "Oh, my."

"I'd burn that." Josie took the letter from her. "It will serve no good purpose."

"It will identify who was in the attic. We have a name, now." She took the letter back. "It could bring closure to his family?"

"Law enforcement would be all over this place looking for the second body. The'd tear it all up." Josie was now looking at the paper that Annie had held as if it were a bomb. "I've seen the shows where they look for bodies. It would be a mess."

"I'll have to think about it, consult a lawyer and give him time to research the repercussions?"

Tom gave her a ghost of a smile before frowning. "While you do that, what about all these ledgers?" He pointed to them as if they were poisoned. "If someone got ahold of that, they might try to confiscate the *'illicit gains'*, which might be this house and all that goes with it."

"So much to consider." Annie stuffed her fist in her mouth, hoping not to cry.

Josie put the letter down. "Might it be possible, Tom, to tell the police the name of the man found in the attic without telling them how we found the name?"

"They will certainly ask. I have to think about it. We don't want to be charged with obstruction of justice. If we withheld information pertinent to the crime, we might be in trouble."

Josie looked at Annie, then turned to Tom. "In the TV law shows, they do subpoenas, and search warrants. Can we hide these where we found them?"

Annie ran her hand over the ledgers "I'm glad we found them, but then again, I don't want trouble. I don't even know what these all hold that might show that my great grandfather was a mobster, money launderer, or at least working with crooks."

Tom took her hand off the ledgers. "I'll talk to one of my buddies who does criminal law and won't know the particulars of this case and see what he thinks. Joe is great at what he does, but doesn't know a lot about criminal law. And he might put two and two together." He looked Annie in the eye. "We'll sort this. Then decide the best course of action."

The Topped Toff

"I'll see if I can make sense of the finances in the ledger. He left them for a reason. He secured them for some reason."

"This is better than a TV show." Josie gazed down at the contents of the two safes. "Let's get this all back into here for now. I'll help." She then started stuffing things back in the safes willy-nilly and closed the doors. "There. Out of sight, out of mind?"

Annie tapped on the safe. "I suppose that it's all irrelevant, all this time later. Lucien died in the early '90's. Those involved are gone, too. His assistant Todd is gone. Kelly Marie is gone, Anita, even my mother is now gone."

Tom gave a nod to Annie. "We're here for you."

"Thanks. I couldn't have asked for better friends." She gave Josie a hug and then Tom. "I think I smell chicken stew. Oh, gosh, I'm not sure I can eat. I feel absolutely off my head. All this family history."

"Or family histrionics." Josie chuckled.

As they left the room where the safes were, they were soon all chuckling.

Tom followed the two women down the stairs and to the kitchen. "At least we know who the topped toff in your attic was."

"Spoken like a writer," commented Josie. "I'm starved. Glad to eat something I didn't have to cook, too."

As they gathered around the table, Annie set out the supper. "I hope to never, ever find another body. I hope there are no more hidden on this property. Or anywhere else, for that matter."

"Agreed," said Josie. "I wouldn't want to find one. Solving mysteries makes my head hurt. I don't even watch mystery shows on television."

As the three were serving themselves, they were chuckling and laughing at the preposterous idea of another body.

≡   ≡   ≡

##

Scan QR code to go to author page on Amazon,

Or go to

Amazon.com: Louy Castonguay: books, biography

Books under Louy Castonguay
   Keeper Series
My Neighbor's Keeper B07K6WQTX6
Child's Keeper B07RTPLSHR
Twins' Keeper B086KY2PCG
Teen Keeper B08FMX466K
Volunteering Keeper B091BDZLMK
Wildlife Keeper B095XQGT2N
   The Lakeside Dower House Series
The Topped Toff
The Chilled Corpse
The Drowned Damsel
   Aunties B&B Series
The Empty House B09B6F8VRC
The Hallow Wall B09TV2FGYP
Weddings B0BKYPD7RC
Kinfolk B0BRQSH6LG

   Books of Short Stories
Let Me Count the Ways B08T6PQVC1
Life Choices B09T8RYXYV

   Books under the author name Lou Cast
Horse Rancher's Quest, B0BX72ZP6X
Erru, the Levite, B0C5S3QLYR
Maria's Choices B0CLJ3XXML

These are all available in Paperback and eBook. For digital readers, click here for author page for any of the books and click on follow.

 Please leave a review here, to help others find this book, if you liked it or go to author page.

Louy is a double graduate from University of Maine Farmington, a BS in Community Nutrition and a BFA in Creative Writing. She has done many types of work and now is a full time writer.
She enjoys quilting, writing, and cooking for others, not always in that order. You can reach out to her at louycwriter123@gmail.com Enjoy this book, and the other books listed.

Made in the USA
Middletown, DE
21 December 2024